the STORY THIEF

Shari McNally

Bella
BOOKS

2014

Bella Books, Inc.
P.O. Box 10543
Tallahassee, FL 32302

Printed in the United States of America on acid-free paper.

First Bella Books Edition 2014

Editor: Katherine V. Forrest
Cover Designer: Kiaro Creative, Ltd.

ISBN: 978-1-59493-413-1

About the Author

Shari McNally grew up in the Mojave Desert where she languished until she made her noble escape at age 19 to Los Angeles. She is married to the most stunning woman in the world and has two demigod children that walk on clouds. This is her first novel.

For Gina, Dakota and Noel
always

Acknowledgments

Thank you to my wife and children, Gina, Noel and Dakota, for their intelligence, humor, love and support. Thanks to Patricia McNally, Michael McNally, Elisabeth Nonas and Pam Tompkins.

Thank you to Bella's fine production team.

My sincerest heartfelt gratitude to my editor, Katherine Forrest.

Special thanks to the 1970s.

Cinderella,
Knight to the Queen

I met the Rebel Queen in 1975, the first week of our freshman year. She was playing volleyball in the girls' gym. I sat in the bleachers and watched the junior varsity team run through drills—serve, set up, spike. I don't remember why I was there. A schedule screwup? I really can't remember. What I do recall is her wearing a loose-fitting sweatshirt and tight shorts that showed off the long stringy muscles in her legs. I can remember the wickedness of her beauty, the way it mocked those around her. And her long blond hair, beyond straight it was so straight, like a beacon in the dark. She was light and everyone else was shadow.

When the bell rang the Queen walked over to where I was sitting and introduced herself with brown shiny eyes that made me think of hard candy, the flavor of root beer.

"Renee Hammond." She extended her hand.

I had never, in my whole life, been offered someone's hand to shake. I took her hand and shook it, awkwardly, loosely, like a rag doll. "Ella Armstrong."

"Ella? So you're Cinderella? I knew there was something different about you. I've read your story, you know."

I'd never had anyone that I didn't know from a young age guess my true name. Everyone always accepted Ella without question. I couldn't speak. I wanted to tell her not to call me that, but I couldn't. All I could say was, "That's not my story."

* * *

My mother had glass slippers made on my sixth birthday. I remember her face when I unwrapped them. She smiled at me with a gluttonous hunger and said, "For my beautiful princess."

I tried to walk in them, but they didn't bend. I could only shuffle. My father was annoyed. He was watching football. "She can't wear those. It's a story. You can't walk in something made of glass."

"What do you care?" my mother snapped back and the daily fight began. "You can't stop watching football long enough to celebrate your only child's birthday."

I tuned out my parents' fighting and wandered out of the room. The slippers hurt my feet, but I didn't dare take them off. My mother's happiness was so fleeting and fragile, I did whatever I could to make it last.

I didn't really think about what I was going to do as much as I felt what I was going to do. I wandered into my parents' room and looked up at my father's sword collection. I unhooked the lowest one and held the weighty length of it in my hands. Once unsheathed, the sword was much lighter. I could hold it with two hands and make it slice through the air. I stood in front of the full-length mirror and posed in a warrior fashion. Now the outfit was complete. The party dress and petticoat, with the glass slippers, were set off perfectly with the glint of the blade. I swung the sword through the air, slicing all evil to shreds, vanquishing all nightmares, until only the good remained, protected by me, the chivalrous Cinderella.

I didn't see my mother enter the room behind me. When she screamed my name, I naturally swung around. I didn't feel the blade strike her as much as I felt the blade stop wobbling in my hands—the contact created stillness, a terrible steadiness. I dropped the sword and the hilt landed on one of my glass slippers, shattering it.

My mother grabbed her thigh and stared at me with her mouth open, but unspeaking, and I saw the blood soak through the material of her knock-off Jackie Kennedy Chanel dress, down her thigh and past her knee. She looked at me carefully, her eyes taking in my dress, looking down at my shattered glass slipper before moving on to the sword. There and then, that was when her eyes changed. When her eyes met mine again, they left me forever. In that moment, my mother was gone from me, from our home, even as she still stood there in front of me.

My father rushed into the room and everything after that was a blur, the bloody rags, the hospital, the thirteen stitches my mother needed on her thigh, the lecture my father received in the emergency room about displaying weapons within the reach of a child.

I apologized over and over again to my mother, in every way I could think of—softly, loudly, dramatically, sincerely. I positioned myself in front of her, held her hand, wrapped my arms around her, but nothing I did could persuade her to look at me.

I disappeared. I was dead. A ghost. She could no longer see me.

The next day, when I came home from school she was gone. My father was sitting on the couch, the same spot he always sat in, holding the remaining glass slipper, doing his best to explain the inexplicable. "I'm sorry, Cinderella, but your mother isn't quite right. This has nothing to do with you. It isn't your fault."

I was young, but I wasn't stupid. I knew I wasn't what she wanted me to be, and that's why she left. I grabbed the glass slipper from my father's hands and threw it at the wall. It shattered so easily it was as if it was destined to shatter, as though it was waiting patiently to be put it out of its misery. "Don't ever, ever, ever call me Cinderella, ever again."

* * *

When the Queen asked me to go to break with her and get a Coke, I was surprised. I don't know why she asked, and I don't know why I accepted, since we'd never set eyes on each other before. But this is the way stories happen when you're young. There are no preconditions or pretexts necessary, unlike the adult years where all meetings are weighed down with the necessity of cause and reason.

We connected right away—in that way that makes you feel like something really *right* is happening—and that afternoon we went to her house, to her art studio/bedroom, and I saw her paintings. She was an artist, and her paintings were vivid and brilliant, primary colors that demanded attention. It became my lasting impression of Renee: vivid, brilliant, primary.

We became best friends, not slow and sure, but in an explosive event.

It was the beginning of my life as a new character, detached and removed from the Cinderella story of my parents.

It was Renee who woke me up, pried my eyes open, and made me see life for what it was—a chosen narration—and she was the ray of light that would carry me through that perilous story to the end. I was now Cinderella, Knight to the Queen.

CHAPTER ONE

Anarchy
1978

Close to the beginning of our senior year, Renee orchestrated the painting of a mural. It was a sneaky midnight art attack—as usual, outrageous and politically driven—painted on the side of the high school administration building. It was the Rebel Queen's fourth art attack. Previous murals included covering an outside wall of both gyms and the cafeteria. Her current high school record now showed two suspensions and, to add insult to injury, the murals were painted over each time. She and Principal Monroe were at war over the so-called art. He saw her creation as vandalism and she saw his response as censorship.

Renee had worked all night. The mural was littered with abandoned cars, odd and even numbers scrawled upon them. It represented the odd-even system of gas rationing (if your license plate was odd-number you filled up your gas tank on odd-numbered days of the month, while even-numbered plates were only allowed to fuel on even-numbered dates) and it spoke to the fucked-up order of things. There was a scathing commentary on California's Proposition 13 and the school programs it axed while saving our parents from high property taxes. The summer session would be literally extinct now and Renee memorialized the losses from basketball classes to drivers education. She painted a not-so-flattering picture of Howard Jarvis and Paul Gann, the architects of the proposition that would bleed our schools dry. Included were lyrics from The Runaways, The Sex Pistols, and Patti Smith. She orchestrated the project, creating the core sketch, and other kids from her art class helped with the painting. The other arties were never caught because Renee made them leave before dawn. But Renee, as their leader, was interrogated each time and suspended. She wouldn't name names and never allowed anyone to take the fall with her. Still, not one of her fellow arties ever stepped forward.

Everyone else went home a few hours before dawn. Renee was left, finishing it up, and Patty was acting as lookout. I came early to help with the clean-up. I wasn't talented enough to actually help with the painting so I was hiding paintbrushes and other incriminating articles in my locker when I saw Patty running toward me. I knew something wasn't right by the disastrous look on her face. Her hot iron Farrah Fawcett curls drooped around her face as testament to the long night.

"Ella, they caught Renee! They just dragged her off to Monroe's office."

"No way! " I slammed my locker shut. "Who would be here this early?"

"Mrs. DeBurgh. Figures that weirdo would come to school early. I mean, really, does she even have a life at all?" Patty huffed while tying to pat her curls back into place.

Mrs. DeBurgh was the history teacher. Her husband died two years ago and she wore his clothes every day. Every day she taught in her dead husband's clothes, and they hung on her as if she were a child playing dress up. Most people made fun of her, but I always felt a little sorry for her. Maybe other people felt that way too, but they didn't show it. I was always a little nauseous when I was in her class. Her despair made me feel claustrophobic. I couldn't distance myself from it, and it emanated from her like cheap cologne that threatened to suffocate us all.

I imagined Renee, quite contained in her capture, not letting on in the least that it shook her, climbing down from the ladder, paintbrush in her teeth, to see Mrs. DeBurgh waiting for her. She probably chastised Renee repeatedly, searching for some signs of remorse between pulling her too-big trousers up higher so she could walk Renee to her punishment.

"How long until first period?" I asked.

Patty looked at her *Lady and the Tramp* watch. "Another hour and a half."

"Shit." I paced and shoved my fists into the shallow pockets of my skintight jeans. I felt Patty's eyes on me. "Okay, I have a really far-out fucking idea."

We ran around to the front of the school to where Principal Monroe's office was located. Patty hung back as the lookout (a role that she was relegated to regularly) as I pushed my way through the bushes to peek inside the window. The room was dark and it was hard to see anything, only Monroe's desk and the closed door. In the corner, on the floor, I spotted my Rebel Queen. Her knees were pulled up to her chin and her arms were draped across them, her forever-determined chin resting on her forearms.

I tapped on the window. She turned and looked in my direction like she had grown bored waiting for me. A pair of pitch-black Vuarnet sunglasses shielded her soft brown eyes. She was always hiding the softness of her eyes behind a pair of sunglasses.

Renee got up off the floor and walked to the window. It was old and all she had to do was turn the lock and slide it up. I know Renee, she did this purposefully slow. Once it was open, she pushed the black frames back, scooping up blond hair as she did so. She leaned on the ledge to tease me. "Come to my rescue, have you? So dependable, my loyal Cinderella."

She knew she was the only one I allowed to get away with calling me that. Anyone else would have been punched in the nose.

"Fine by me, I'll leave you here to rot." I turned and walked back through the bushes.

"You? The pure of heart? My loyalist knight? Ella Armstrong, you get your ass back here!"

The thrill of her voice firmly saying my full name stopped me in my tracks. I turned, but held myself cool and composed. "And why should I help an ungrateful bitch like you?" The hint of a smile curled at the corner of my mouth.

An unexpected laugh was bestowed upon me, the loyal knight, but it turned into a pout almost as quickly. "Seriously babe, what am I going to do? My parents are going to shit."

I walked back to the window and put my hand on her arm. "I have a plan. Just sit tight. And don't ask me what it is—you'll ruin the surprise."

Renee dropped her head below her shoulders, shaking it over my nerve. But it was my win. I'd gained her confidence. "Okay, fine, don't tell me, but may I remind you it's my ass on the line?"

"Just hold on to your ass 'cause I'm going to blow this place sky-high."

"No shit?" She chuckled, not believing a word I said.

"Sure am, all you have to do is sit pretty and go along for the ride."

She put her hand over mine. "We both know you're always my best shot at liberation." With a lopsided smile, she added, "You always have been."

"Foxy and a flatterer. Will wonders never cease?"

She didn't lose her smile as she walked back to the corner. She sat down and pulled her legs into her chest. She was a mystery to me. Sometimes as mighty as a giant, other times as delicate and fragile as a china figurine, as she seemed to me now.

I made my way through the bushes, taking the ANARCHY button off my shirt, along with the other half-dozen buttons that marked me as anything less than good girl. "Come on, chick," I told Patty. "We have some phone calls to make."

* * *

I watched my plan unfold as the cameraman panned to get a full shot of the mural. A prettied-up woman reporter talked to him, while another less beautiful print journalist talked to the students gathered around the painting, his photojournalist vying for space with the roving cameraman. By then the news had spread and there wasn't a single student in class, every one of them trying to figure out how to get on TV.

I'd snagged the local paper, but my big score was getting the local television station from Los Angeles to make the dull trek through the San Fernando Valley, over the hills, to the Mojave Desert, the embarrassing stepchild of Los Angeles County. LA didn't know we existed until October 1977, when the space shuttle Enterprise landed at the Mojave Desert's Edwards Air Force Base. I've always wondered if that was part of the reason they agreed to cover the story. We were, for a brief moment in time, interesting. I hooked the press with the promise of radical politics, juicy censorship, and thrilling student protests against Proposition 13.

Monroe came out of his office with various teachers following behind. He was trying to be casual about the reporters and the students going wild trying to get on camera, but nervous red blotches covered his face. When the plastic woman reporter approached with her polished nails glistening like the claws of a predator, Monroe shook her hand like a zebra in a pack of hyenas.

"We received a call about this wonderful mural," she practically crooned, "and wondered if we might talk with you and some of the artists? Bobby," she called over her cameraman. "Let's get this shot set up." While the reporter was busy setting up her shot, the print journalist saw Monroe and ambled over, a look of weariness on his face. He fired questions at the principal. "This anti-Prop 13 mural is very admirable considering it won't be popular with many parents who approve of the property tax protection that Prop 13 provides. What was the process of allowing the students to have a voice about something that so clearly impacts their education, and whose idea was this—a teacher's, a student's, or does it represent the school administration's stance?"

"Well, I, uh," Monroe stuttered.

I gave Patty a shove forward and she took her cue. "It was Renee's idea," she said.

The reporter turned to look at Patty—his new source of information. "Can I get a last name?" he asked.

"Hammond. She thought up the whole mural idea, including the theme, but she never could have pulled it off without the help of Principal Monroe. He's been so supportive and generous with his time." Patty smiled sweetly at Monroe and batted her eyes at him.

The reporter looked at Patty suspiciously. "When the call came in, we were told this was a controversial situation—a case of censorship. If your principal isn't censoring you, who is?"

Patty waved my hook to the press away with one dismissive hand gesture. "Oh no, not on Principal Monroe's part. But this poor man, the student's hero, has to do battle with the school board, parents, PTA mothers...I mean, really, he's the most popular principal in the history of the school. Everyone loves Principal Monroe!"

I clapped my hands together firmly, shaking my head in emotion. I motioned for the students around me to join in.

Mrs. DeBurgh came forward and eyed Monroe. "But Principal Monroe, I was under the impression you knew nothing about this!"

"I, uh, well...the thing is..." Monroe continued to babble.

"What? Not know?" Patty was incredulous. "He's been the very foundation of this project. As a matter of fact, he was only keeping it from the rest of the school as a surprise." That might have been pushing it.

The reporters and DeBurgh looked at Monroe. Patty's face was immobilized in a smile. I wasn't sure how much longer she could endure it.

Monroe finally broke and laughed nervously—not confirming it, but not denying it.

The reporter nodded and wrote that down on his pad.

Mrs. DeBurgh looked at Monroe with disdain, pulled up her oversized trousers and wandered off, mumbling to herself.

"Can we get an interview with the artist?" the TV reporter asked.

"Yes, can we talk with her please?" asked the print journalist.

"Sure," Monroe said, "I'll go get her, I know just where she is." Monroe laughed nervously some more. He seemed more like a self-conscious teen than the kids who surrounded him.

Moments later, Monroe walked out escorting Renee by the elbow. Renee pulled her arm away from him but he just took it again rather firmly with a pained smile and whispered something in her ear. The reporters gathered around her but didn't say anything at first. Stunned by her looks, most likely. Her fair skin and blond hair swam in a sea of black clothing. Her girl-next-door looks with her pretty blond hair, as it streamed down her coat to the middle of her back, warred with the dark clothing and darker attitude. Her black boots and leather pants, Sex Pistols T-shirt, the safety pin hanging from her ear, made her look a little too much like the teenage badass that all adults feared worshipped Satan. In theory everyone wanted to root for the bad girl, but only as an ideal. And unlike the cutesy version of good-girl-turned-bad-girl that was Olivia Newton John this summer in the movie *Grease*, Renee was the real deal. And no one, most especially an adult, was keen on experiencing the actual physical reality of that ideal in the flesh.

As the reporters asked her questions, I leaned against the wall and soaked up the visual before me. They—the reporters, the teachers, Monroe, the kids standing around—were all so animated. But the Rebel Queen, she just stood there with an expression like the Mona Lisa. I wondered if any of this meant anything to her. This coup was due to her mural and her dogged persistence. Did it make her happy? Sad?

She looked in my direction. I couldn't see her eyes, under those dark Vuarnet sunglasses, but I knew she was looking at me because she smirked.

CHAPTER TWO

The Queen's Court

We were watching second period action of the boys' playoffs. Now, watching basketball is not something I'm usually inclined to do, but Patty whined and pouted until Renee and I both agreed to go.

The bleachers were half full with people watching the game and half full with people talking among themselves. It was a meeting place for socializing and people watching. That accounted for all the activity off the court. Half the time you couldn't see the game because someone was standing or walking in front of you—headed for the snack bar, the bathroom, catching the attention of a friend who just arrived. Even the people who came specifically to watch the game would often give up and give in to the chatter.

Ricky Hernandez had his arm around me. I stole a glance at his profile. He had sharp features that framed the smooth lines of his face. I looked on my other side where Renee coolly leaned back against the next row of benches. Next to her was Patty, who sported the quintessential look from the JC Penney catalogue. She leaned forward watching every move Paul Rand made on the basketball court. Every time he moved her eyes moved with him. The girl was caressing his body from afar.

"Patty, your eyes are gonna pop out of your head," I observed.

She rested her chin in her hand and never took her eyes off him. "Isn't he a stone-cold fox?"

I shrugged. Paul Rand was gorgeous if you liked perfection, but I liked bumps and quirks. Give me an all out superb bod and I'll raise my brow and whistle, but give me someone with a crooked nose, too full lips, some cute physical imperfection, then you've got me. My heart thuds faster and I'm much more likely to fall in love.

Ricky Hernandez's features were too angular for a model's, but he made me feel safe when I looked at him. He was quiet, rarely said a word, and I liked that.

"Oh God!" Patty bemoaned. "I *have* to go to the dance with him! I want to get my hands on that cute little ass! Can you imagine him in a pair of Angel Flights?"

"Patty, do shut up already. It's getting old." Renee said it wearily, not even bothering to look at her. The antithesis of Patty and her love for disco clothing, such as the Angel Flight pants the boys wore out to the disco, Renee wore punk clothing, plaid tartan bondage pants and self-made T-shirts from her silkscreen classes. Safety pins, buckles and straps all figured prominently. I leaned toward Renee's style but couldn't be bothered to go out of the way for the look as she did. I often wore self-made shirts and jerseys, but I was lazy with my pants and often just wore the same ripped up jeans.

Patty sat back, her spirit broken. It was always like this when Renee chastised her for being too exuberant. She looked up to Renee, not that she wanted to be like her (I don't think anyone, including Patty, could imagine that) but because Renee was something Patty would never be—cool and aloof. The problem was that Patty believed that Renee's ways were superior to hers. And so she gave in. Always.

And that was high school in a nutshell. The broken, angry, hurt kids were too afraid to show their emotions. That's what cool was all about. And because they had little regard for their lives they were risk takers—they became the trendsetters, deciding in their reckless way what would be cool and what would not. And all the kids with the functional family lives, with safety, love, support, would follow their damaged peers off the cliff to their respective ruin. This seemed so obvious to me. Patty was the only functional one in our group, but she still tried to be like us. She never seemed to realize we were like that because we were trying to survive.

"Has Monroe said anything to you about the mural?" I leaned back next to Renee.

"He hasn't spoken to me since *The Incident*." She spoke as though fiendish organ music accompanied her words.

"So, does this mean he's not going to suspend you?"

"I guess there's a first time for everything."

"It's been nearly a month. One of your murals has never been up for that long."

Renee sighed. "I know." She sucked on her top lip and looked a little worried, but in moments her expression changed to amusement. She pointed to the floor of the gymnasium and chuckled. "Look at Chad Walker trying to impress our dear Rapunzel."

She meant Diane Lacey. There was a time-out on the court and Chad Walker was waving and smiling to Diane Lacey, until the coach popped him in the back of the head. I saw Diane among the cheerleaders and seeing her there with them, I thought what I always did: it didn't make sense. She wasn't like the others. Patty, with all her exuberance, would have made a better cheerleader than Diane.

Diane was remote, her smile to the crowd almost apologetic. But even so she seemed to belong there—maybe because she was so beautiful, simply the most beautiful girl in the school. Not like Paul Rand was beautiful—all perfect—but, well, I guess she was *inner* beautiful. Though she was pretty on the outside, what with her wavy brown hair and an all-American smile, it was Diane Lacey's ways, her difference from others that made the entire school worship her. Unfortunately for her, it was that same difference that kept most people at a distance.

Something about Diane was too good, too modest, too 1950s sitcom good girl, and it made people nervous and awkward around her. Maybe it was because she came from such a strict family. She was never allowed to go anywhere except for school. No one really ever got to know her. That's why Renee called her Rapunzel.

"You know," Renee said, "Walker's the only guy who's ever had the courage to go after Lacey."

I watched Chad strut and prance about the basketball court for Diane. I watched Diane not know he was alive. "I guess he's a pretty talented athlete." I couldn't think of anything nicer to say.

"All that God-given talent and he's still just another dipshit," Renee deadpanned.

It was true. Chad Walker was undoubtedly the biggest jerk I'd ever met. I laughed but came up short when I saw Larry Altman and Gerrard Daniels sit down behind Renee and Patty.

Renee looked at Altman and sat up stiffly. "Where the hell have you been?"

He tried to kiss her cheek but she pulled away as he laughed. "I was with Gerrard. Right, Gerrard?"

Gerrard looked uncomfortable and didn't answer. It didn't matter because Renee didn't even look at him—it was beneath her dignity.

"I don't give a fuck," she said under her breath, "if you say you're going to meet me—then do it! Otherwise, don't waste my time."

"Sweetheart!" Altman acted victimized, placing a hand over his wounded heart. "I just lost track of time!"

I turned to look at Altman and his big, bulky, football self. He was one of the few guys in school who could actually grow thick sideburns, and there right below on his neck was a red lipstick mark. I looked at Renee's naked lips, then back at his muscular neck.

"Hey, Altman, looks like something's made a nasty bite on your neck." I gave him my best leveling glare.

His eyes narrowed and a slow smile formed on his lips. "You know, Ella, I did feel something bite my neck, just a few minutes ago, on my way over here. Some foxy little bug must have found me irresistible." He took the collar of his "I'm too cool" suede jacket and wiped the lipstick away, never taking his eyes from mine.

"Really? Well, if I were you, I'd start wearing turtlenecks. It's mosquito season, you know, and you wouldn't want to catch any diseases."

"What the hell are you two talking about?" Renee looked at me with eyes that were one-part hurt and one-part annoyed.

"Nothing." I could feel Altman's eyes burning a hole in my back. I soothed my anger by telling myself that one day I would catch him at his game.

Why they were even a couple was beyond me. Altman was mister jock, mister look at my cool sideburns and my tight bellbottom pants. What was Renee thinking? I know she didn't give a shit that he was popular. So what the hell did she like about him? He was charming, but so obviously an asshole and a player. I swear he thought a spotlight followed him wherever he went and the entire world was his audience.

"No, Gerrard!" Patty lowered her voice, "I don't want to go out! I've said no a million times! What do I have to do, hire a plane and write it in the sky? Look, I don't want to be a bitch, but how many times can I say no?"

We all looked at Gerrard. I thought sure he'd crawl into himself. Christ, I would have. For a moment he looked embarrassed but then he leaned forward and whispered to Patty, loud enough for us to hear, "Your voice says no, babe, but your eyes say yes. You know, I can only wait so long before my interest wanders elsewhere."

I don't know if Gerrard was saving face, or if he was suicidal and didn't have the nerve to do it himself.

Patty's hand balled into a fist and her face turned red with anger. Renee put her hand over Patty's fist and turned to Altman, imploring him for assistance. But Altman, his chest and shoulders heaving in repressed laughter, was no help.

I looked at Ricky but he simply rolled his eyes and shook his head.

Renee pressed forward, her face just inches from Gerrard's. "Take a fucking hike little boy. You catch my drift?"

In school, you can be in the same space with someone hundreds of times and never actually speak to him or her. I don't think Renee had ever spoken directly to Gerrard before that moment.

Gerrard stood, a little too macho for his small frame, and touched Patty on the shoulder. "Let me know when you change your mind. I can't wait forever. Later, babe."

I suppose it was a matter of pride.

Gerrard edged his way to the aisle and Altman laughed out loud and threw a paper cup at him. He called him an idiot, in that way boys have of savoring other boys' screw-ups.

The buzzer rang and it was halftime. The crowd stood up and the cheerleaders ran to a box filled with small rubber basketballs. They started throwing them up into the stands. People were diving for them, laughing as the balls whizzed past them barely out of reach.

I stood there, not really expecting to catch one, when I saw Diane Lacey smile at me. I smiled back, and when I did, she threw one right into my hands.

CHAPTER THREE

Mere Mortals

Damn if I wasn't in my senior year, having to go to school only part-day, yet the stupid assemblies and the insipid pep rallies always seemed to fall during second or third period when I was still on campus.

The gym was completely full and the cheerleaders were doing their best to whip the crowd into frenzy, but no one seemed in a good mood as we sat blowing illegal bubbles with our gum and gambling with our extra change.

I was sitting up in the bleachers with Patty and Renee. I was playing the odd and even game with Patty and had already won a dollar fifty. Patty and I would toss a quarter in the air, catch it, and then hold it covered on top of our hands. If the coin faces matched—tail and tail or head and head, it was even. If it was head on one and tail on the other, it was odd. We took turns calling odd or even and whoever won kept both quarters. Patty lost six games in a row on the assumption, and diehard hope, that if she kept calling even it would eventually turn up. I, on the other hand, always trusted my luck with the odd.

I was getting pretty bored with the game when Monroe finally started reading off the names of the people voted onto the prom court. That was the purpose of the lame assembly after all. That, and to excite the student body about some athletic event that no one cared about.

Being a gentleman, Monroe started with the girls and the first two oh-so-special contestants, and confirmed princesses, were the Cartwright twins, both cheerleaders, that Renee and I had dubbed Itsy and Bitsy. Truly, I didn't even know what their real names were. We all sat there bored out of our skulls while they hopped around and did those ridiculous jumps cheerleaders do when they get excited. They reminded me of little dogs that peed on themselves when they got too worked up.

Next Monroe called out Diane's name—nothing odd about that. Diane was a cheerleader, she was well liked, a pretty traditional pick, but something was wrong. I realized it was Diane's lack of enthusiasm. There were no cheery jumps, no smiles. She just stood there, taking it, like she was waiting for a blindfold and a fucking cigarette. It was actually kind of hilarious and I think I laughed out loud.

Monroe went on, "…our next princess nominated to the prom court is…" He looked at the list a moment too long, hesitating before he announced, "Ella Armstrong."

My chin dropped down to my chest, I'm sure of it. I felt nothing but the pounding of blood in my ears, though it was soon accompanied by a slight sense of nausea.

Renee looked at me as her eyes widened.

"What the hell?" My voice cracked in defense. My first analyzing thought surfaced and I struggled to understand why I would be chosen. Why me? I was no Barbie-Brain casualty. "I don't know anything about this," I blurted defensively. "I thought, you know, only cheerleaders could be these things. Isn't there some rule about that? Some bylaws? Something…"

Monroe patted his brow. He meant to get on with it, but something stopped him. He kept looking at the sheet of paper he was holding. He cleared his throat and with clear reluctance, said, "And our final princess is Renee Hammond." He said it fast and quick as if that would make it go away.

Renee's lips actually turned white from the pursing of her lips. She pushed her aviator glasses back farther on her nose. She crossed her arms over her chest and her foot rocked with highly agitated rapidity.

I just couldn't believe it—first me, and now Renee? What the hell? I knew people respected and feared Renee but I didn't think they saw her as Queen-for-a-Day material. Not the type of Queen this required her to be. She was the Rebel Queen. An outlaw. She was certainly pretty enough, but most people were afraid of her—I mean, she was fairly hostile most of the time, which, call me funny, doesn't seem like the characteristic you look for when you want to plop someone on top of a float. Plus, I mean, this was the girl who'd started nearly every campus protest for the past four years. Protests most kids only joined to get out of class, mind you. I mean, only the fringe really understood most of what she did. So what was this? A joke? Maybe it was because of Altman, him being such a jock and all. Maybe it was all a setup like in the movie *Carrie*. And when the sparkly title of Prom Queen was bestowed upon us, a large bucket of pig's blood would be ceremoniously dumped on our heads as our final high school humiliation. The problem was we didn't have Carrie's telekinesis powers, so we couldn't destroy the insipid shallow tyrants of our high school—thus, there would be no satisfying, however fantastical, vigilante retribution.

I looked at Renee and saw that she wasn't going for the idea. Christ, how does one remain the Rebel Queen, retain her edgy dark antihero status, while being crowned a prom queen?

Monroe's piggy eyes fixed on Renee and bled disapproval. If he had his say, some troublemaker like Renee would not be on the court.

"This can't be for real," I said.

What people apparently didn't understand is that they'd paid us the ultimate insult by nominating us to something that we considered trite and shallow. To accept the titles would be to become what we scorned.

Patty tried to smile at me but her smile kept drooping into a pout. She was the only one of us who would have actually enjoyed such a traditional honor. She would have acted as if it was unimportant, but she would have secretly eaten it up with a spoon.

"If you girls will come down front so we can present you," Monroe instructed.

"Present us? What are we, French poodles at a dog show?" I stubbornly crossed my arms with no plans to budge. "No way am I going down there." My head was working, trying to figure a way out of this disaster, when Renee leaned over and whispered into Patty's ear. Patty frowned and nodded while Renee went on, occasionally gesturing emphatically. Finally, Renee stood and descended the bleacher steps.

"What? What are you doing?" I was appalled. How could she? "Are you crazy? You're going to accept this...this...*archaic* bullshit ritual?"

Renee looked over her shoulder at me and nodded, indicating I should follow and trust her. I was not at all convinced. "Oh, come on!" I called to her. I moved about in my seat undecided for the first time in my life about whether to follow Renee's lead, but it was true that she had never let me down before. I sighed and begrudgingly got to my feet. I walked down the steps after her, but sulked the whole way.

On the gym floor, the auditorium looked huge. I was no longer concerned about my outrage because I had stage fright. It felt like a million eyes were on me and I froze.

Monroe mumbled something and everyone applauded. My fingers went numb and my underarms started to itch like mad. The next thing I knew the Cartwright twins, one after the other, were talking into the microphone and saying things I couldn't comprehend because my heart was beating so loud in my ears.

There was a pause. I looked around. Everyone was staring at Renee as she stepped up to the mike.

"You don't have to do this anymore." The auditorium was dead silent. "Why are we up here and not you? We're not any better than you are. They keep doing this to us. Trying to make us fit into this mold of placing some of us above the others. It's already hard enough. We have to come here every day and suffer the humiliation of high school. And we can never break out of it because the school itself participates in separating and dividing us. But we don't have to do it anymore. We can stop it now. When the ballots come around, put your pencil down. Don't vote. Refuse this stupid, fucking tradition. Tell them to shove it up their ass!"

Principal Monroe leaned forward and barked, "That's enough, Miss Hammond!"

She walked off the gym floor toward the exit. The burst of applause and hooting was deafening.

I approached the microphone and tapped on it as wads of paper flew past my head. My voice cracked and I hesitated long enough to clear the lump in my throat. "I won't participate."

As I walked away I could hear the pounding of feet on the bleachers getting louder.

I heard Diane's amped-up voice. "I decline too." The girl who surely would have been the queen, and everyone knew it.

She must have been right behind me because by the time I got to where Renee was standing, Diane was at my side.

Monroe and the twin cheerleaders stood there dumbfounded. Itsy's and Bitsy's heads were tilted like a couple of alert cocker spaniels.

Monroe finally spoke into the microphone, "That's enough! Quiet down! If anyone else throws something, they'll be in my office! There's no need for mayhem! We will get the names of the runners-ups and have a new court announced. During third period you will vote for the prom king and queen—"

"Why do we need a king and queen?" Someone up in the bleachers called out loudly. "Can't we celebrate without having to worship *mere* mortals from our own peer group? It's not like they're supergods and were mere humans. Everyone here matters! No one is any more important than anyone else!" It was Patty yelling out and gesturing over at us.

The student body bristled, became unruly. The kids got it. Why did they always have to feel less than? People turned and started talking to each other. Many voiced agreement. Why did they have to do this thing? Because it was a tradition? And was that a good enough reason anymore? Maybe all of it was just stupid and pointless.

"No more idols!" someone yelled.

People started standing up and clapping. Someone started chanting and others joined in until the whole crowd was shouting, "No more idols! No more idols! No more idols!" My laugh was pure astonishment. Everyone was protesting and Monroe couldn't shut them up. For one shining moment they were bigger and more powerful than him.

Then I saw Altman. He wasn't clapping or chanting, but looking past me with dark, dead eyes. He let down his defenses and I could see into him, into the person he really was. The chilling coldness I felt from him unnerved me. Assuming he was giving Renee this stare, I turned to say something to her, to warn her, but the heavy door to the gym was closing slowly on its hydraulic hinge, leaving only Diane and me.

"Come on, Lacey, let's get your delinquent ass out of here."

Diane lifted her eyes to me as her cheeks reddened. I noticed that her eyes were brown and yellow mixed together—they were golden. She bowed. "After you princess."

I laughed in astonishment for the second time that day. I curtsied, my fingers plucking at my ripped jeans. "You're too kind, your highness." And I stepped out into the bright light of an early afternoon, nothing but freedom on my mind.

CHAPTER FOUR

Same Stupid Story

"It was an honor just to be nominated." Renee laughed at her own joke.

We were at the Taco Stand eating tacos. It's where everyone went on the weekend to hang out, but we were there in the middle of the day because we'd left school after the assembly. "Are you sorry, Cinderella? After all, it was your chance to be the Princess at the Ball."

Why did she say these things? To annoy me? "Fuck off." It hurt my feelings.

Renee realized she'd taken it too far. "I just mean…is there a part of you that wanted that story and I took it from you? I guess I wasn't really thinking about that—I feel sort of bad."

I thought about my mother, which I didn't like to do. I played with the straw in my Coke and thought about her and what my being a princess would have meant to her. "For a moment, I wished my mom could know." If she knew I was nominated to the prom court, that I was a princess, would she come back home? Would she love me again? You know, would she stop being so disappointed in me? "It doesn't matter. I'm never going to be whatever it is she wants because sooner or later she'll see I'm not a princess."

"No, you're Cinderella—knight in shining armor. Cinderella, slayer of evil and thief of hearts."

Patty laughed, glad that Renee made the conversation lighter. "Thief of hearts? Who's heart has she stolen?"

"Mine, for one," Renee said.

I felt my cheeks redden.

"She keeps it hidden in a jar buried in her backyard." Renee was looking at me too seriously. I couldn't hold her gaze and looked down at my taco. "That's why I'm so heartless."

It was enough to break the ice. Patty laughed and so did I. I played with my french fry, dipped it in the ketchup and drew a heart with it. "If I only played that princess role she wanted me to play, some part of me would have to die. Am I willing to die inside to make her happy?"

"Stories can change," Patty said. "You can be the knight in shining armor and the princess."

"I don't know. I've thought about that," I said. "It seems a bit like trying to shove a square peg in a round hole. It's like all those feminists talking about the princess stories and how there should be a story where the girl doesn't need to be rescued anymore, you know, she's in charge, she rescues the prince, or doesn't need the prince, or whatever, but it's all the same vibe. Why not just make up a different story all together? Why keep trying to tell the same stupid story over and over again?"

"Because that story is a part of all of us," Renee said. "We all want to be rescued at times."

Patty looked at her with the same surprise that I'm sure was on my face. When did Renee ever need rescuing?

CHAPTER FIVE

Ain't Nothin' But a House Party

Renee and I strolled up the front walk to Lanky's house party. Since it was late fall, everything surrounding the house was dead. Grass. Trees. Bushes. Even the rickety two-foot-high wooden fence that corralled the yard looked as though someone needed to put it out of its misery. Not even weeds grew in the yard. It was a sanctuary for the lifeless.

The house was situated out in the boonies, the next house a mile down the road, so no one worried about how loud the parties got. It was only an hour since the sun had set and the party was cranked up to a bass beat that made your insides move like Jell-O. Lanky's parents were a little backward—some people joked they were cousins, though I'm pretty sure that was just a rumor—and they seemed to believe that drinking parties for teenagers were just a natural part of life.

Before we walked through the door, Renee turned and smiled at me in a self-mocking way that no one else ever saw. Other people thought Renee took herself too seriously. I knew she didn't, and I sometimes wished someone else besides me would see it because it made me feel lonely and a little crazy.

The inside of the house was dark and black lightbulbs threw spooky shadows across the walls, illuminating shabby furniture and bad art. David Bowie was humming through the house. He was singing that he was the king and the girl he loved was the queen and that for this one solitary day they could be heroes.

The music was so loud that to talk to someone you had to yell just inches from his or her ear. I was accustomed to these parties and knew the next day my voice would be hoarse and my ears would still be ringing.

A fog of pot smoke hung in the air above everyone's head, mixed in with cigar smoke and a few cigarettes. The eyes that turned to me as I passed were red and dreamy and the smiles slow, as they nodded to me as languorously as buoys floating in the water.

I spotted Ricky kicked back in an armchair, a beer in his hand, his feet crossed on an old, peeling ottoman. When he saw me his face turned from a pose of cool aloofness to one of warm affection. He opened his lap to me and I sat down, giving him a soft hug and kiss. He reached into the ice chest next to his chair and handed me a cold beer. I opened it and leaned back against him and we watched the scene around us in quiet companionship.

My eye caught Renee at the entrance of the hallway near a gaudy velvet picture of a bull and matador. She was talking to Jimmy Zimmer, "Zip," a friend of Altman's, and I knew immediately that Altman had flaked again, and I wondered if he knew he was pushing it with Renee. For a moment, my mind zoned and it was like I could feel Renee's hurt, her anger and embarrassment. As Zip moved past her, Renee looked up for an interested moment at the velvet bull before walking down the hall to the back of the house.

Patty was crossing the room toward me, her face lit up and animated compared to the stoned ones all around me.

We smiled and hugged as though we hadn't seen each other in years. We did this because this is what we always did—I don't know why. It's like, in the teenage years, you think every action was on some stage where you were perpetually watched. She kneeled down next to the chair, grabbed my thigh and shook it.

When she finished shaking my leg, she let her hand rest there affectionately.

"Hi Ricky," she said.

"Hi Patty," Ricky murmured.

"Paul Rand is here," Patty said to me with another excited shake to my leg.

"Is he?"

"Yeah."

I wanted to tell her to be careful because I knew Paul would use her, and what Patty was really telling me, between the lines, was that she wanted to *be with him.*

What that meant differed person to person. To Patty, I sort of guessed, it probably would be anything short of actually sleeping with him. And I couldn't tell her to be careful, or that Paul Rand might not care about her any more than he would a fucking blow-up doll—that would be unsupportive. And being unsupportive meant, *you aren't a real friend or you'd understand,* and that led to silence, and the next thing you knew was you didn't know jack shit about your friend, or if you even still had a friend. So, I learned to let people make their mistakes. Besides, who knows, maybe Patty wanted to be used. And anyway, wasn't she using Paul for the way he looked?

"I was going to go talk to him, but Laura Jameson is hanging on him like a leech! I think he wants me to talk to him because he smiles at me when I walk by. But I don't know…"

I faded out. I knew this scene well. I wasn't a friend at this point, just a wall.

Out of the corner of my eye I caught a flash of red. I glanced over and saw one of those old-fashioned red cloth Windbreakers they wore back in the fifties. I looked down farther to a pair of jeans pulled over military boots. Fascinated, I looked up to see the guy's face. He was looking directly at me. My first reaction was to look away but something in his cool, stoic expression invited me to study him further. His brown hair was spiked up, the tips painted a bright green. A semi-beard grew on a jaw that tapered softly, making his face appear sensitive, and his eyes were strange, like dark tunnels, pulling me into them. In his right ear he wore a safety pin.

"Ella?" Patty asked, shaking my leg yet again.

I jumped and spilled a small amount of beer on my abused leg.

"Do you think I should go talk to him, or not?"

"Yeah, go talk to him! Jesus!" I was edgy, the way you get right after you've been scared and feel stupid about it. "Hey, wait. Who's the guy in the doorway?"

Patty looked, but I made it a point not to.

"What guy? There are a million guys here."

"The punk with the red jacket and the spiky hair."

"I don't see anyone like that."

I turned and looked. The doorway was empty. "He was just standing there."

"I'm gonna go talk to Paul. Wish me luck."

I looked back at the doorway, but he wasn't reappearing.

"Ella, you have to help me."

Gerrard stood in front of me with pleading eyes.

"What are you talking about, Gerrard?" I was ambivalent about Gerrard. He hung around with Altman and tried to act like him. He needed to get real.

He leaned closer. "Patty," he said, "I like her a lot. I don't know what to do." He cut his eyes at Ricky then whispered in my ear, "How can I make her like me?"

"Stop being such an asshole for one," I said, "and stop being so desperate."

Gerrard knelt down next to me. He looked at me with hope because he thought I had some magical answers. "What do you mean?"

"I mean stop trying to act like Altman. It doesn't work. Also, everybody's desperate about someone, but some people hide it better than others. You, Gerrard, do not hide it well at all." I laughed.

"I don't?" He looked concerned.

"Look," I said, sitting up and getting into it, "you don't want the person you're desperate about to know because it weakens your chances."

"It does?" He looked around to make sure no one would discover his desperation.

"Sure," I said with conviction. "Say you're desperate about me and I know it—I'm loving it. It makes me feel good and avenged for all the times I was desperate and miserable about someone. You keep being desperate, Gerrard, you're screwed. Right, Ricky?"

Ricky nodded. "Screwed."

I looked past Gerrard's shoulder then because I couldn't seem to keep my eyes still. My eyes strayed across the room, through the doorway and into the kitchen, where Diane Lacey struggled with Chad Walker, who had her by the wrist.

"I have to take care of some business," I said, dismissing Gerrard. I gave Ricky's leg a squeeze and went to help Diane.

I made my way past several groups of people who wanted to get me high and were holding out various incentives. By the time I reached Diane and Chad, he had her around the waist, her body pulled into his. She was pressing her hands against his chest, trying to get free, but he was much stronger and not letting go.

I walked up to him, as cold as could be. I wanted my face iced. Chad saw me coming and he loosened his grip on Diane. As soon as he did she pulled away.

"Chad, man, you need some fucking manners." I pulled Diane toward me. "Do you know this girl? Obviously not, or else you would know that you don't press Lacey."

Chad raised his hands, palms showing, to indicate he had backed off.

I led Diane away. The only reason Walker let her go was because we were at a party where I had a lot of friends. If she were ever completely alone with him, she'd be in way over her head.

Diane held my hand as we left the kitchen, and she held it so tightly it scared me. When I turned to look at her she seemed ready to cry.

I pulled her into a dark corner of the room, away from other people, so no one would see her like that. If I were walking across a crowded room with tears in my eyes, I'd be embarrassed as hell.

"You know Chad's a total prick. You shouldn't go near him. What's the matter?" I held her by the shoulders and made her look me in the eye. "He didn't do anything to you, did he?"

Diane shook her head and looked at me with her golden eyes. Her expression was funny, I mean, really strange. I couldn't read it.

"Thank you," she said and hugged me really tight.

The next thing I knew she was skirting her way around the groups of people rooted through out the house, making her exit out the front door.

I stood there completely confused by Diane's departure. An uncomfortable, unsettling feeling dug deep into my bones, and all at once I had the sense that everyone in the room was staring at me, like I'd fallen into a thick, sticky barrel full of self-consciousness. I looked around but saw no one was paying any attention to me, standing alone in some dark corner.

Well, almost no one. That strange new guy reappeared in the same doorway and was grinning at me through a river of smoke and bobbing heads.

"To the dashing hero!" He raised his cup to me. "You rescued the princess!" He had a self-satisfied smile that was as irritating as it was unnerving. Like he was sharing a secret with me.

The only thing was, *I* didn't know what the secret was. I turned away and looked at anything else but him and his mocking smile.

CHAPTER SIX

Rapunzel

I had a dream Mom came back. She was making breakfast and Dad and me were sitting at the kitchen table, laughing and talking with her as she brought us eggs and bacon. It was like a TV commercial where everyone was perfect and happy and there was a dog that looked like Lassie and I had a brother and sister and we were fighting, but I still loved them, and I'm part of something bigger than just me. After I woke up, it took me a while to feel...

The phone rang, which caused me to jump and my pen to fly off the page. I jumped at the phone and answered it like it was a bomb I had to disarm.

"Shit...Hello?"

"Such language! I oughtta wash your mouth out with soap. I was thinking, my fair Cinderella, do you want to go to the Ball as outlaws?" Renee's voice always had a tired-out familiar tone, like we had known each other longer than our time on this earth.

I leaned back from my desk and my journal. I looked at the painting on my wall. The one Renee painted for me as a joke:

Woody Allen on a surfboard riding a tremendous blue wave, white nose-coat on his face, his rage against a backdrop of sun and fun. It looked like one of those cartoonish self-portraits sold at street fairs. Over the summer I became obsessed with *Annie Hall*. Renee swore it was because I was smitten with Diane Keaton's wardrobe, but it really had something to do with that life. I wanted to be Alvy Singer or Annie Hall and have friends that talked with sophisticated wit. I wanted my life to have cutaway vignettes that encapsulated the humor and irony of each episode of my life. Mostly, I wanted out of the Mojave Desert.

At any rate, I could do what I wanted with my room because I didn't have parents telling me I couldn't. After my mother left, my father became more and more detached. It was like he wanted to forget the whole marriage and kid thing ever happened. Now he lived with some woman I had met a few times and saw on holidays when my father felt too guilty not to spend time with me. Since I didn't have any brothers or sisters, since it was just me, maybe it was a little easier for him to forget I existed? Most kids thought it was great that I didn't have parents breathing down my neck. I guess it was good in some ways. And my dad was never mean to me when I did see him. I just never saw him that much. The worst part was when I would get lonely, or a little afraid. I didn't get scared all that much though, only when I heard noises I couldn't figure out. And Renee and Patty came over a lot, so that was pretty cool. Their parents didn't know that my dad was never here because we all lied about it. Not that I like to lie, but I just hate it when I see that look on another parent's face—that pity look. I just hate that so much. It makes me feel ashamed and exposed and pathetic, I guess.

"Western or modern outlaws?" I asked.

"Come over, we'll talk."

* * *

Renee's bedroom was part studio. The walls and ceiling were completely covered with images and canvases were stacked everywhere, some done, some half done, some painted over and ready for something new. She was in the process of something new and had only just begun.

"What's this going to be?" I asked.

"Not sure. I can't talk about it yet."

And she couldn't. I knew this about her. She wasn't putting on airs. Just, sometimes, some things weren't finished in her head.

I flopped on Renee's bed, the only stick of furniture in the room besides a dresser and an antique wooden chair cushioned in red velvet, which no one save Renee sat on—it was hers. Renee claimed very few possessions but those she did claim, she held on to tightly. Her bedroom had a large closet, at whose far end was a small door that led to the bathroom that had been built by Renee when she realized she had no desire to be in any other part of the house but her bedroom. Thus, she needed only to paint, sleep, and relieve herself. As for food, meals were a more complicated war that had been on going between Renee and her mother for years—battles were won and lost depending on the entrees and the morale of the soldiers.

Plus, though it was never discussed, Renee didn't get along with her father. I was around him more when we were younger. He wasn't very nice to her. He was always ragging on her. And I don't mean about her clothes, or music, or the regular sort of parent gripes. He was always criticizing her intelligence, always trying to make her feel stupid. Once, a few years ago, when she was asking to go out on a date, he actually called her a stupid whore. I heard him say it. He told her she was just going to get pregnant like her mother did. Renee's parents had married their senior year of high school because Renee's mom was pregnant with her. I always thought it was weird they didn't have any other kids. It was like it happened, Renee arrived and time stopped, leaving him in a perpetual state of anger. And what more can be born from that? Anyway, I really hated him, but I never told Renee that. Nowadays, I never saw him because the only way I ever entered the house was through her bedroom window. I think Renee's mother knew when I was there but she never bothered us. I think she was trying to protect us from Renee's father by not telling him when I was over.

I picked up the snow globe that sat on her bedside table. Inside was a cherry bomb. I shook the globe and watched the snow fall on glitter-dome mountains (like granulated sugar) and on top of, down and over the sides of a plump, ripe cherry bomb. I loved that freaky globe. It was wicked cool, and I always played with it whenever I was in Renee's room. It was such an odd little thing. Renee made it in an art class after hearing the Runaways' song "Cherry Bomb."

I picked it up. "I so dig this."

Renee looked at me, very serious. "Tell me why."

I shrugged. "I don't know. It's just so..." I shrugged again. "It reminds me of that song by Neil Young 'Sugar Mountain' but like if Cherie Curry was singing it." We both bent over and laughed in that way people do when they think it's funny, but they know no one else would.

We sat for a while and didn't really talk. We were really good at being able to share silent companionship. She was the only person I knew that I could do this with—most teenagers wanted to yap obsessively.

Renee methodically washed her paintbrushes in a basin of muddy water. She concentrated on this as if nothing else existed. Her fingers smoothed and rubbed the bristles as I watched. The slow sureness of the movement comforted me, sending me into a peaceful state that felt timeless.

At home in her studio, Renee had an uncomplicated look in her baby T-shirt and tight black pants covered in paint, her hair pulled back from her face except for a piece that played hide-and-seek with her eye. Seeing Renee this way made me realize people really looked their best when they weren't trying so hard.

"Shit, we're already modern outlaws...let's be western outlaws," Renee said.

"What?"

She moved the hair from her face and looked at me patiently. It took me a minute.

"Oh, for the dance, you mean."

"Or we don't have to go at all. Please, let's not go, Ella. Shit, we can think of something better to do then go to some stupid-ass high school dance."

"I already told Ricky I'd go, not that he'd care much, I suppose. What's the deal with Altman?"

"I don't know, what *is* the fucking deal with Altman?" Renee asked, though it was not a true question.

The phone rang and Renee turned back to her painting, palette in hand, ignoring the ringing. I hung off the side of the bed and frantically searched through a pile of clothes for Renee's phone. I finally found it underneath a pair of overalls with fresh paint all over them. My hand was now a bright shade of green.

"Hello?"

"Ella?"

"Patty?"

"Ella, is that you?"

"Patty, is that you?"

"Stop it!"

"Stop it!"

"I mean it, Ella! If you don't stop, I'll scream! I have serious business to attend to."

There were times that I enjoyed being immature way more than I should. I couldn't find a cloth to wipe the paint off my hand. "As tempting as that is, I wouldn't want your mother to institutionalize you."

"Okay, go ahead and tell me, I can take it."

"Tell you what?" Each cloth I found had fresh paint on it.

"What did Renee decide for the dance? She certainly wouldn't be caught dead in a formal, someone might mistake her for a normal person!"

"Well, now that you mention it, we were just discussing dressing as western outlaws."

"Outlaws? Western? You mean, like bad guy cowboys?"

"I don't believe I've ever heard anyone cover the definition quite so thoroughly."

"Ella, this is the Winter Ball! How am I supposed to get out of the house, and past my mother, in a pair of chaps?"

"Tell her you think an afternoon of goat roping would be just the thing to relax you before the big event. Shit, where's a clean cloth, Renee?"

"How can Renee do this to me? She knows I'm going to the dance with Paul! He'll never go in costume. Ella, what am I going to do? Can you convince her to go as something else? Ask her, would you Ella?"

Renee tossed an old stained T-shirt to me, but at least it was free of fresh paint. I wiped the paint off, but it had sat there too long and some of the green wasn't coming off. "Shit, damn paint."

"Please, Ella!"

"Okay, okay, I'm asking, hold on." I covered the receiver with my partially green palm. I knew Renee was following my half of the conversation but she continued to mix paint. I waited until she faced me.

"Is Patty whining?" Renee asked.

"She was hoping for something more traditional," I said in a low voice.

"Does she honestly think she has to wear what we wear? Does she honestly think I give a shit what she wears?"

"Renee," I said, lowering my voice even lower, "you know she looks up to you in some twisted Sandra Dee way that I don't quite understand, but she does look up to you."

"Fuck that shit. I don't want the responsibility."

I gave her a scolding look. "Now, now, my evil Queen, you know you love being worshipped."

She held her paintbrush in a way that made it look as though she were going to paint the air. "Is that what you think I am?"

"What? No. I'm just kidding."

Renee threw down her brush. "Let's get out of here. I need air."

Renee already had her tattered black leather jacket on and was putting her hair up under a newsboy cap. She pushed on the glass pane, the window swung open, and she jumped all of three feet to the ground.

"Bye Patty, call you later." I could hear Patty still yelling at me as I slammed the receiver onto the hook in my haste.

I went to get up and my hand landed in a container of orange paint. "Oh, come on, man!" Afraid that Renee would get too far ahead of me, I hastily wiped off the paint with a small clean corner of the same stained T-shirt and rolled off the bed, scrambling to follow her out the window.

* * *

The sun had set during our walk. We'd passed an elementary school I didn't know the name of, but had walked by a million times, when Renee abruptly stopped.

I was half a house ahead of her when I realized she was staring in the window of a small, weather-beaten white-planked house with a cherry tree in the front yard. Light came from one particular bedroom window and lay upon the yellowing grass. I walked closer to find out what mysterious ritual was mesmerizing the usually unflappable Renee. "It's Rapunzel," she said, with a bit of awe.

The object in the window came into view. I heard music playing soft and muted, classically beautiful. Long wavy hair defied gravity and swirled around to keep time with graceful limbs. Elegant whirls and sweeping gestures filled the open room, corner to corner the body flew around easily. My mind filled with words I had heard but didn't understand: pliés, gran ban ban, pique turn.

Ballet. Poetry of the body.

It was the rarest, most superior thing I'd ever been ambushed by, and I felt a burning as it was branded upon me in a permanent memory.

"It's Lacey," Renee said.

Diane Lacey? I was seeing the movements as large and without parts. I looked closer to see the parts that made the whole, and no doubt it was Diane's face, Diane's intense expression that showed through the big movements.

Some inner voice in my head gushed at how lovely it was and how there must be something almost divine about Diane for her to dance so beautifully. But my admiration made me feel silly. "We're invading her privacy. We shouldn't be watching."

"You don't understand. Lacey hides everything wonderful about her. It's time that stopped." Renee said to me as though I were a child, "Watch your Evil Queen now."

Renee walked across the dead grass. I lagged behind her with no intention of catching up. She tapped on Diane's window. I held my breath and cringed as Diane's dancing stopped so unnaturally.

"Rapunzel, Rapunzel, let down your hair!"

Diane was surprised and a little frightened. She took a few steps backward until there was recognition on her face. Then her gaze dropped to the floor, closing us out in embarrassment. After an awkward moment that seemed to stretch on for an eternity, she walked over and opened the window.

I felt the heat come at me. A balmy wall made up of humidity, light, and the sweet smell of the healthy body. Diane's breathing was labored, whether by the workout or nerves, I was unclear.

"You scared me," she said and pulled at the curly hair stuck to her cheek. "What are you doing here?" She looked at Renee then past her at me. She pulled at the straps of her leotard though they were positioned properly.

I felt a gigantic urge to put her at ease. "We were taking a walk, that's all. Next thing we knew we were in front of your house, so we decided to stop and say hi. Right, Renee?" I poked Renee between the shoulder blades. Each poke said, *Be nice!*

"Well, we were on a walk, but it was your dancing that stopped us."

Diane picked up a towel and pressed it to her face. I'm sure it was to cover her expression.

"Don't be embarrassed. It was wicked. I had no idea you could dance like that. I hope you take it seriously?" Renee asked.

"Well...I don't know..."

"You really should, Lacey. Don't you think so, Ella?"

"You dance really nice," I offered lamely. "I don't know a lot about dancing, but you seem awfully good."

Diane tried not to smile real big, but she did smile some and continued to wipe her neck. "Do you want to come in?"

"What about your dad?" Renee asked.

"It'll be okay if you're really quiet."

We climbed through. I was as quiet as I could be because we had all heard tales about Diane's dad—overprotective is what people said. She was the ultimate Daddy's girl. She could do no wrong, but he wouldn't let her do anything—and I mean *nothing*. I had never seen her, in all four years of high school, at any sort of party or hangout place. Diane had only just been allowed to go out and she was in her senior year.

I had never been in her house before, but then neither had anyone else that I knew of. Her room was impeccably clean. Her bed was pushed against the wall to create more dance space. An old stereo played some kind of classical music. The floor was wood, which I found intriguing, as I'd never seen a wooden floor in real life. (Everyone I knew had ugly carpeting, except for Patty's house. They actually had white carpeting. How stupid was that?) Then it struck me that the floor, the dancing, might have been the trade-off for her imprisonment.

Diane changed the music to a cassette tape of the Talking Heads and cleared her bed of a few stray clothes so we could sit down. She dumped the clothes in a clothes hamper and walked in a fidgety manner across the room to the window, closed it and stood nervously. The next thing I knew, she had stopped the cassette and turned on the radio. Van Halen was covering the Kinks "You Really Got Me." I think she was trying to figure out what we wanted to hear, like we would judge her based on her musical selection. I noticed she had the soundtrack to *A Star is Born* leaning against a pile of records. I wondered who she was really. What did she listen to when she was by herself? Streisand? The Talking Heads? Was she a New Wave girl? I had a sudden urge to really know who she was underneath that good girl facade—was it real or was it Memorex? I watched her cross and uncross her arms, dividing her glances between the wall, the floor, and us. Her high-strung behavior had me so uptight that my shoulders were up about my ears. Obviously Diane wasn't used to having guests.

"Damn Lacey, we haven't come here to assassinate you," Renee said bluntly.

Diane's cheeks turned a rosy red.

I punched Renee discreetly on the thigh and received an impish grin. Renee was having a good time. I saved Diane from Renee by changing the subject. "Did you like the movie?" I gestured to the album.

Diane relaxed for the first time and picked up the album of *A Star is Born* with Streisand and Kristofferson naked and embracing on the front. "It's my current favorite."

"Mine too!" I leaned forward, excited.

Renee looked at me in a way I knew meant I was hurting her. "I thought it was *Annie Hall*?"

I shrugged. "I can have more than one favorite."

Diane said, "What's your favorite scene?"

"When the moving man accidentally turns on the tape recorder and Ester hears him singing and she goes running through the house…"

Diane sat on the floor in front of me and finished my sentence. "John Norman! John Norman!"

Renee gave us a haughty look. "Seriously?"

It was my favorite movie last year. I saw three different matinee showings all by myself because I knew Renee didn't like it. "Just because you don't like that kind of music doesn't make it a bad movie."

"I love all Streisand movies," said Diane.

"I loved *The Way We Were*. For some reason I always remember the scenes about the key to her apartment. Like when she first gives it to him, he salts it and puts it in his mouth. Then later, when it doesn't work out, he sets the key on the table between them and it's so sad because you can feel her heart break. Oh my God, that scene killed me."

Diane was looking at me, carefully, without speaking. Something was churning in her head. I could feel it. The emotion accompanying it was something I had never felt before. It felt like adoration or love, but that couldn't be right. We barely knew one another.

Renee got up and walked across the room. I looked over at her and saw that she was annoyed, but something else too. Jealous maybe? I don't know because the look was gone in seconds.

"So," Renee said in an upper-class, uptight Connecticut accent, "Diane, are you going to the big dance? Since, obviously, you can dance."

Diane shrugged, not looking Renee in the eye. "I don't know. Chad Walker asked me."

Renee walked back over to the bed and sat down. She leaned forward in disbelief. "Just because the fuck face asks you doesn't mean you have to go with him."

"No one else asked me," Diane said, as though that would explain it.

Plainly, she didn't know Renee that well.

"Christ, Lacey, that's because you're so unapproachable! Why don't you just go alone? Or better yet, why don't you ask someone that you'd actually like to go with?"

"I can't do that," Diane said softly.

"Why the hell not?"

"Because I...I just can't, that's all."

"That's such a load of fuckin' bullshit."

Diane looked offended, as if she could actually smell the bull's excrement. I wished Renee would stop cussing. Diane wasn't the type of person you could cuss in front of and it was making me uncomfortable.

"Bullshit," Renee repeated. "You know what? You can do whatever you want to do, and the only one stopping you is *you*... Rapunzel, locked away in your tower."

For a moment Diane looked as though she might say something important. "I'll probably just go alone."

Renee slapped her hands on her thighs and stood up. "Damn brilliant, Lacey! That's it. We'll both go alone. We'll dance with whoever we want, and we'll fuck whoever we want."

I cringed. Diane wasn't that type of girl. I wished Renee would drop it.

Renee crossed to the window and opened it. "Meet me at my house an hour before the dance starts." Without a backward glance, she jumped down and headed across the yard.

Damn. Diane Lacey and Renee Hammond arriving anywhere together was such a bizarre notion. Just being in the room with them, they were they such opposites that I expected any minute they would annihilate each other's existence.

I was still sitting on the bed, unable to make the transition from park to third gear quite so quickly. Hanging out with Renee was a chore, not to mention how difficult it was to keep my social skills polished. "Well," I said, standing. "I guess we're leaving."

"You don't have to go," Diane said. She looked up at me and I had a snapshot moment—one of those split seconds where your brain memorizes someone and it becomes a picture that you see in your head whenever you think of them. Her curls around her face were damp. A few strands stuck to her red cheeks, and with her head down, she lifted only her eyes, half-mast, and they were shimmering gold. The way she looked at me was indescribable. It was as if some live wire opened between us.

I was straddling the window, one foot in, one foot out. I tried to compose myself, but the lamp shone on her from behind and created a halo of light through her wavy hair. She was magic. I was too shy and wasn't pulling off the cool and aloof that I was shooting for when I awkwardly said, "Rapunzel, Rapunzel, locked away in your tower. Let down your hair and I'll come back and visit sometime."

She smiled. "Okay."

"Well, I'll see you."

I went to swing my other leg over but was so busy trying to be charming that I caught my heel on the ledge and lost my balance. I fell to the ground with a thud.

And there I sat, on my butt, in the dark, underneath Rapunzel's window, completely stunned. The next thing I saw was Diane's concerned face looking down at me. That confused moment seemed to go on forever before the embarrassment hit and I cracked a smile. Diane mirrored my expression, though she was kind enough to try to hide her amusement behind her hand. A laugh slipped out from one of us, and there I sat, and there she stood, both of us cracking up.

"And Cinderella fell out of Rapunzel's window," Diane said.

I nodded, still chuckling, and picked myself up off the ground. I could feel my cheeks burning. I backed away from the window and waved to Diane, who was no longer laughing but now smiling in a way that made me feel timid.

Once I reached the sidewalk, Renee looked at me with a self-satisfied expression and said, "Who's the evil Queen now?"

I grabbed her by the arm and started running so I could feel the adrenaline pump through me. When we finally stopped, the night was dark and silent, except for the moon, which hung like a fingernail clipping in the sky among a handful of stars. It was eerily still. Maybe the stillest I have ever felt under the night sky.

Something felt different. It was like the day after my mom left. I remember walking into the living room, no different than it had ever been, but it was like I had never been in that room before. Like it was hazy or just an illusion before that, but now I was really seeing it. That was the way being under the night sky felt to me. Something had shifted and I was scared but also pumped up inside. My past experience was that something really bad had to happen to get that feeling. What had I missed? What had gone wrong? And why did I also feel amped up?

CHAPTER SEVEN

Tuck and Roll

The prom was held outside in the quad. Fake snow sparkled in the trees, glistened on the ground, and a full moon lit the sky. The DJ played as kids danced in the seventy-degree California winter evening. Because of Renee's rally for a protest of the royal court, not enough people voted for a king and queen to be elected. It was the first time in the history of the school—hell, maybe any school—that no prom court was announced. It was a sublime victory.

Ricky was dressed cowpoke-mod-psychedelic-mumbo-jumbo. Whatever it was, it was a style that I'm pretty sure didn't exist before that night. He was dancing with me, though that was just a technicality. Ricky loved to dance, and because of his quiet nature, it was his only real form of self-expression. He would dance with anyone and, honestly, a partner wasn't mandatory.

I was decked out in my own western attire: Levis, sheepskin vest and bandana, which had all been mysteriously left on my doorstep. In the package was also a poncho and hat that made me look like Clint Eastwood in *The Good, the Bad and the Ugly*, and a long, skinny cigar I was currently holding between my Eastwood-style clenched teeth. Hung low on my hips was a holster and plastic six-shooter. The note accompanying the package:

Cinderella,
Your gown for the Ball.
Signed,
Your Fairy Godfather.

I was certain it was Renee who sent the package, but I couldn't figure out why she would sign it that way.

A lot of other people were dressed in costume with their own slant on Renee's outlaw concept. Patty had found a happy medium by dressing as a barroom madam so she could still wear a dress and get past her mother. The point of our costumes was to thumb our noses at tradition, and she looked ridiculous dancing with a disgruntled Paul Rand who was dressed in a polyester suit, unable to poke fun at himself. He posed on the dance floor as though he hoped *Esquire* magazine would wander by and discover his stunning good looks.

I noticed a girl from my trig class standing off to the side of the dance floor. She didn't have a partner to dance with but her body reacted to the music, so I pulled her onto the floor to dance with Ricky. I figured he'd never notice. She came willingly, not even questioning, and I left the dance floor for fresh air and something to drink.

Bypassing the punch bowl—which I'm sure the football players had peed into—I took a cool drink from the grungy water fountain. I turned back around just as Renee and Diane entered the dance.

Renee didn't look all that different from usual. She was all in black but her hat was western and her boots had spurs. She wore a pair of skintight black gloves that made her look like this wicked bad girl.

Diane stood near her looking innocent and sweet in a western shirt, fringed vest and Levis. Her wavy brown hair sprouted from beneath a tan dress-up hat—the fancy type cowboys wear on special occasions.

I closed my eyes. I had a hard time seeing Renee and Diane at the same time. They were so opposite of each other, and so separate in my mind, the distinction was piercing. It was sort of like imagining Doris Day and Patti Smith hanging out together. An interesting notion, but you just know a duet of "Que Sera" or "Gloria" will never come from it.

Speaking of which, Renee walked over to the DJ and handed him an album. The guy took it out of the sleeve and put it on. Next thing you know, the Patti Smith Group was replacing the Commodores.

I saw an awkward boy approach Diane. Even from a distance I could see him struggle to be her prince charming, but Diane put him at ease, accepting his offer to dance. The boy prince was visibly relieved as his princess walked with him to the dance floor.

The music slowed and Ricky motioned to me. I made my way like a pinball, bumping off the dancing couples, finally bouncing into Ricky's arms.

Not more than two couples over, Chad Walker danced with a freshman girl I had seen before but didn't know. His expression was clearly angry. I looked at what I knew he saw, and there was Diane, dancing with that awkward boy, having shunned Walker to come to the dance alone. His obsession with Diane set off warning sirens in my brain. It was like watching a truck racing downhill without any brakes.

Abruptly Ricky twirled us around and held me close. We both laughed and when I looked up into his face, I saw desire mixed with expectation and I wondered what could make a person feel that way. Why did I make Ricky have that look in his eyes? I wondered if someone knew when they had that look on their face. It occurred to me that I might be standing too close to Ricky, distorting and misreading his intentions. I pulled away and studied him. But now his expression was spiced with that squint Ricky gets when I confuse him. I smiled, and when he smiled back, I leaned forward and kissed him. Because I knew that's what he was waiting for, that's what *the look* was for.

The kiss was comfortable. We knew the routine: his arms around my waist, my arms around his neck, our bodies pressed lightly together. We'd had sex before, but not often, it was almost like we had done it because it was expected of us, and because of that, neither of us pressed each other for it. And that was nice. It made our relationship uncomplicated.

Unexpectedly, a tingle started at the base of my neck and a cold chill ran up my spine. I turned around so quickly that Ricky didn't have time to let me go. I stood with my back to him and his arms still wrapped loosely around my waist. I leaned against Ricky, securing my backside from harm, and scanned the area nervously.

"What's wrong?" Ricky asked.

Couples danced, the music played on, and I stood there afraid, for no apparent reason.

"What is it?" Ricky pressed.

"I don't know," I whispered, still searching for why I was uncomfortable. Then, for no particular reason, I looked up to the top of the building directly in front of me. At first I saw nothing but shadows, but then there it was—movement. I focused on the motion and saw the blond hair. Renee was up on the roof. She was waving to me—no not waving, but gesturing to the wall. It was only a foot lower than the roof, and where she must have climbed up.

"What's wrong?" Ricky asked.

"It's Renee," I said, "she needs me...or something. I don't know."

Ricky smiled regretfully, but not begrudgingly. "Go to your bad girl."

I apologized with a look before leaving him stranded on the dance floor.

I made my way through the crowd and hoisted myself up onto the wall. It was cake to climb onto the roof from there and the noise that the rock roof would have normally made was covered up by the loud music.

I bent over, so as not to be seen, and ran to where Renee sat, leaning back against the lip where the roof met the wall.

"What are you doing up here?"

She didn't answer me but shrugged. She picked up a rock and threw it.

I moaned and lowered my butt onto the hard edges of the large white rocks that covered the rooftop. I adjusted and readjusted. There was no chance in hell of getting comfortable.

The night pulled around us, and the loud music acted as a buffer between the world and us. I noticed Renee looking up at the full moon like it was a lover who had been lost to her, or some such tragic thing, and I tried again. "Is something wrong?"

"Wrong?"

"Are you dodging Altman?"

She exhaled loudly as though she had not considered that thought until just now. "He pisses me off."

"Why?"

"I don't know. Why does he ever piss me off?"

Renee lowered her eyes. Hiding whatever it was that she didn't want me to see. Her lashes were long and her skin so soft looking. It was amazing to me that she was able to divert people's attention with clothing and attitude. How could they not notice her perpetually pouty lower lip?

"We're going to graduate pretty soon," she said.

"Thank God! I'm sick to death of this place!" I waited for her to agree with me, expecting we would have a satisfying bitch session about high school, but Renee was unenthusiastic.

"I have to tell you something, fair Cinderella." She picked up some rocks and threw them a few feet away. "I'm nervous."

"What about?"

"I don't know if I'll make it in college. I'm scared of being alone."

"Oh, come on. You have a good GPA. You did well on your tests. Why wouldn't you do well at college?"

She shrank away from me. I noticed it but I ignored it. The strange thing was, I felt myself starting to get mad.

She said timidly, "Because I'll be alone. You're going somewhere else."

"Look, Renee, where you're going is a good art school. It's not the best school for me—you know that. We've talked about it all year for chrissakes!" The more we went on about this the angrier I became. Was she trying to make me feel bad for not being able to attend the same school as her? "What am supposed to do with myself at an art school? I'm going to school locally anyway, that's all I can afford!"

"I just don't want to be without you!" Her face was strained and her fists clenched. "Why can't you just listen to me? Why do you have to get so mad?"

"I'm not mad! I just think it's pointless to keep going over and over something that can't be changed!"

A deep voice boomed from below. "Hey! Who's up on that roof? Get down from there!"

Renee and I were looking at each other, still embroiled in our argument.

"Come down right now! Do you hear me?"

The voice brought us around. I saw the recognition of our situation in Renee's eyes as they grew rounder. She jumped up, grabbed me by the wrist and pulled me to the other side of the roof.

Renee looked down. I was scared to look but figured there was no way out of it, so I looked too. It was a long way down. Sure there was grass, but it was a really long way down to it.

Renee said, dead serious, "We have to jump."

"We can't jump from here! Are you fucking crazy? We'll break our legs!"

"Not if we tuck and roll, like they taught us to do in volleyball."

"Tuck and roll?" I was so panicked that it sounded like some kind of jelly doughnut. "Renee, I'm serious, I really don't think—"

She jumped off the roof. Right the fuck off! I couldn't believe it. I had an image of her being a dwarf for the rest of her life. But when her feet hit the ground, she pulled her knees up into her chest like shock absorbers, allowing her momentum to continue, and she rolled onto her shoulder. To my utmost amazement she stood up in one piece. She yelled up to me, "Come on Cinderella, it's easy! Jump!"

"Jesus, Renee! I never took volleyball!"

Renee's face drew a blank, like she just couldn't wrap her brain around this concept.

"I mean it! Get down from there this instant!" This came from the other side of the roof. One of the chaperones was climbing up.

From the ground Renee was motioning to me like a wild woman.

I began to blabber to myself, "Oh my God, oh my God, oh my God!" Thrown back into the rituals of my Catholic youth, I crossed myself frantically and jumped off the roof.

My tuck and roll wasn't quite as good as Renee's. It was more like a drop and slam. For a second I saw birds and heard twerps like I was a *Looney Tunes* character.

The next thing I knew Renee had me by the collar and was pulling me across the grass. It was a good ten yards before Renee graciously decided to grab me by the waist and pull me up to my feet so I could run along next to her instead of being dragged on my hands and knees. My legs felt like noodles as we ran out as far as we could into the dark grassy fields of our high school. It would take a large search team armed with flashlights to find us.

That last thought allowed me the luxury of dropping face-first into the grass. My lungs felt like they'd pop and, when I turned over, I saw that Renee and I were a lot farther out than I realized. The lights from the dance were distant and small.

Renee was laid out next to me trying to catch her breath as well. When she looked at me, she laughed. "You should have seen your face."

My temper rose. Now that I wasn't scared anymore, I was mad. I punched her in the arm.

"Ouch!" She stopped laughing and rubbed her arm. "What the hell did you do that for?"

"Don't you ever, ever, make me jump off of anything again!"

Renee was still rubbing her arm, but she chuckled. "Don't punch me, Cinderella."

I don't know why, it's like I couldn't help myself, but I punched her again, and just as hard.

Renee's mouth fell open. "I don't believe you!" She grabbed my wrists and threw me back onto the grass. She swung her leg over my middle and sat on me.

I struggled with everything I had to free my hands but Renee was stronger. The more I tried to get loose the madder I got. "Get off me," I threatened behind clenched teeth.

"Are you going to punch me anymore?"

"I'm going to keep on punching you until you apologize for almost killing me."

"I did *not* almost kill you! Are you bleeding? Are any bones broken?"

"When you let me up," I promised both her and me, "I'm going to punch you."

"Well, I guess you'll never get up. Not ever. We'll just stay here for the rest of our pathetic little lives. They'll find our bony skeletons years from now, in the same fucking position, and all because you're the most stubborn person I've ever known!"

That did it.

I pushed as hard as I could, a huge surge of energy. Renee was thrown off balance at first but she quickly regained it, keeping my wrists pinned to the ground.

Seeing there was no hope, I stopped trying to get loose. I let my body go limp. I unballed my fists and turned my head to the side, diverting my eyes. I wouldn't look at Renee because she had defeated me. The Queen defeating her Knight? I was humiliated.

Renee loosened her grip on my wrists but she kept her hands softly there. It was a strange moment because I knew I could have gotten free but it was like there was this peace in me, and I imagined I was a deer, the hunter's rifle aimed at me, and this feeling of piercing clarity, knowing I would die, came over me. Then there was acceptance. A strangely peaceful acceptance, that's what I felt. Fine, let the Queen kill me. I accept my death.

Then Renee's fingers gently grazed my palm and everything went blank. Something big came up from my stomach and lodged in my throat. Replacing my calm was sudden horrific fright as immediate and startling as if a concrete block were dropped on my stomach. And I knew, knew without doubt that if I were to look at Renee, something dark, something that had never seen the light, would be there. And then, oddly, it was Ricky's face I imagined and that wanting expression of his that had fascinated me earlier, and I realized that was it, that's what I was afraid to see in Renee's eyes. And just as quickly, part of me wanted so badly to see it. Because I knew that's how she was looking at me. I knew it with certainty. I wanted to know how would that look be on Renee's face. Directed at me. Did the Queen love her Knight that much? Did she want to kiss me? Just as my curiosity was rising up to overcome my fear, I realized it was too late.

It was over as quickly as it came.

Renee moved off me. Her weight was gone. At first I felt some relief, but it was soon replaced by a tidal wave of regret. What an idiot. Why didn't I look at her? I'd made a huge mistake. Out of the corner of my eye I could see her sitting on the grass next to me.

"I'm sorry if I hurt you." Renee's voice was low and more intimate than usual.

I sat up and had the most unusual sense of my own body weight, like I'd just returned to earth from outer space. "Just my wrists." I rubbed them for effect.

"And you have my official apology for almost killing you," Renee said, trying for just the slightest sarcasm. But you could tell her heart wasn't in it.

I tried to smile but couldn't.

"Ella," Renee said in a way that meant I should look at her.

I dreaded it, but I looked at her. In her eyes was some kind of hurt I'd never seen before.

"Don't be mad at me," she said, almost pleading.

"I'm not. I'm really not mad." And I wasn't. But whatever replaced mad was curious, and made my head hurt, and I wanted to cocoon myself and fall asleep. "Should we go back? People are probably wondering where we are."

I knew Renee wasn't ready to go back when she plucked a blade of grass and pulled on it. She sucked on her top lip, her profile a pout. "What people? What difference do they make?"

I almost took it back, said let's not go, let's stay here. But the moment was gone. I took the hand she offered me and we walked in silence.

Halfway back Renee put her arm around my shoulder and kissed my cheek. When I looked at her she smiled in her charming way, just like the old Renee would have done. But in some way she was no longer the old Renee anymore. Something between us had changed, some point met and passed. I smiled weakly. I could see in Renee's discouraged expression that she knew it too.

When we reached the front entrance to the dance Renee stopped.

"Aren't you going in?"

Renee shook her head. "I'm way beyond the Ball, Cinderella. Will you give Rapunzel a ride home for me?"

I nodded. I didn't want to give anyone a ride anywhere. I didn't want to go back into the dance either, but there were Ricky's feelings to consider—though he probably hadn't really missed me.

Renee was indecisive for only a second before she put her arms around me, hugging me to her tightly. Her silky hair comforted one cheek while the rough material of her jacket scratched the other. I hugged her longer than I had ever hugged her before, beyond good manners and ignoring shyness. And when we did part I turned my face toward her just enough that the edge of my lips brushed the edge of her lips, very slowly and delicately, and then I was looking at her. She touched her lip with her black-gloved hand where I had grazed it with my own. She reached up to my mouth, to my lip, almost touching it, then stopped. Instead she held my hands and stepped back away from me with searching eyes, like she was looking for something there that she needed to see even as she was pulling away from me, until our hands parted. But I don't know if she found what she was looking for, maybe she didn't, because she turned from me and walked away. I kept watch of her until she disappeared into the night, her long black jacket and long golden hair catching the wind. She was a true fairy tale Queen. There was no other like her and I knew there never could be.

I'd never felt so left, or so alone. Even though I was alone a lot, it was my first deep sense of loneliness.

As I turned to go back into the dance, I saw that new guy standing near the entrance, smoking a cigarette and dressed like the Marlboro Man. He leaned against the wall, arms crossed, his eerie eyes watching me. "Did the Queen like your ball gown?"

I looked down at my clothes. "That was you?"

I walked toward him and he smiled—a stupid, knowing smile. One that let me know he had been watching Renee and me. I felt embarrassed. "Why? Who are you?" I asked.

"I'm your Fairy Godfather, of course."

"What?"

But he just smiled. "Don't worry," he said, "the story's not over yet. In fact, it's just beginning." He held up a homemade wand with a cardboard star on the end covered in glitter. He touched the wand to his lips and when he blew a kiss, glitter billowed toward me.

I'm not kidding.

"Okay, you're just weird." I walked past him and his unwelcome predictions, back into the fake snow and loud music, nursing some sort of heartbreak that I didn't understand.

* * *

I had a dream that night that I flew through the Queen's window. I was dressed in armor and wielding a sword.

She was in a black dress with a queen's crown and she was painting her bedroom walls black. The paintbrush she used was mammoth size and it nearly didn't stay upright in her hand. She struggled with it as she stroked back and forth, back and forth, leaving a thick coat of black paint until the room began to shrink.

Across the room a spotlight turned on, its directed beam falling into a chasm in the black paint, absorbing all the light so there existed a continuum of light falling into a black hole, into some sort of nothingness.

The Queen's hair was pulled back into a ponytail and, where her neck met her shoulder, a small drop of perspiration appeared. It moved slowly, with stops and starts, curving across her collarbone, gaining speed and following a path between her breasts.

I dropped my sword and frantically lurched toward the drop, like it was a matter of life or death. But instead of capturing the small drop of perspiration, I found myself holding a glass slipper.

There was an ear-shattering crash behind me and, terrified, I spun around, my heart thudding so loudly the beat of it filled the entire black, shrinking room. I saw a dark figure dart for cover to escape my sight. When I turned back to the Queen, I saw she was fading into the black paint, becoming more and more distant. I reached out to rescue her, but my hand hit the wall with a loud crack and the glass slipper fell to the floor, shattering into splinters.

CHAPTER EIGHT

Pod People

One day, during the snack break between second and third period, I was going to a food stand across from the cafeteria when I saw a chanting crowd coming out the double doors of the lunchroom. I forgot about the doughnut I was going to buy and walked over to see what was going on. As I got closer, I heard them chanting Principal Monroe's name. Then Renee stood up on a bench, hammering her fist and encouraging them to be louder. A lump formed in my throat when I saw Monroe round the corner with his security—an old frail guy named Crane, and a big dumb guy named Benji. They were both worthless because you could outsmart one and outrun the other. God knows I did it enough times. Renee saw them coming too and quieted the crowd, which was the only reason I was able to hear Monroe ask what was going on.

"These people want their right to expression. We want the mural you destroyed repainted." Renee stood with hands on hips.

I was surprised. I didn't know anything about the removal of the painting. Monroe had played it smart and waited just long enough for us to forget about the too-political mural.

"We won't budge until it's agreed to. That means none of us will go to class, right?" she questioned the crowd and the kids replied with upheld fists and a roar.

"The school board cannot allow the defacing of school property. And it is not art—it's an editorial! It's too political and not appropriate for a public school." Monroe was trying very hard to be authoritative.

"You call art a defacing of property?" She looked at the crowd, appalled. "Well, I call your destruction of art a perversion, and this school an institute of fascism!"

There were two stoner guys in front of me. One leaned over to the other, "What's fascism?"

"You know," the other said, "too many kids are a slave to fashion, man. I think she also called him a pervert." They both laughed.

I stood on my tiptoes. It was getting hard to hear because there was a buzz as people began to talk among themselves. I saw big, dumb Benji reaching for Renee. She pulled her arm out of his reach and yelled over the group, which was becoming larger, "Sit down! Everyone sit down!"

Amazingly everyone did. As soon as people in the front sat down so did everyone else. It looked like a domino demonstration.

I sat down behind the stoner guys. The bell rang for class and there was a nervous twitch throughout the crowd. It just goes to show how programmed we all were.

Monroe broke. "All right!" He was obviously going to do whatever was necessary to get us to class. "I'll consider it. But you're going to be suspended for starting this disruption," he said to Renee.

"Fine," Renee said. "Do we have a deal?"

"No promises."

Renee turned to her followers. "Stay seated!"

"Okay!" His face was heart attack red. "The mural can go back up...*under supervision*."

Renee gauged his sincerity and stood up. "You can't renege or we'll start up all over again."

Monroe turned his attention to the rest of us. "Get up, and get to class! You're already late and your tardiness will not be excused."

Kids started standing, none too happy, mostly because they had thought they were going to get out of class. The protest was a disappointment to them.

The crowd dispersed around me. I pushed through people until I was where Renee had been standing. I saw her just as she rounded the corner with Monroe. I picked up my pace and trotted after them.

I was just turning the same corner when I ran smack into that guy who said he was my Fairy Godfather. I almost fell on my ass but he grabbed me and steadied me. He had that ever-present amused smile of his.

"You again! What is it with you?"

"Cinderella, dressed in yella, going to save her...Rebel Queen?"

I looked down at my yellow T-shirt. "Go ahead and call me that again and I'll punch your face in. Why are you always watching me? What the fuck business is it of yours what I do?"

"Oh, let's just say I have a vested interest."

I admit it. I was suckered into his I-know-something-you-don't conversation. "What are you talking about?" I looked over his shoulder as though I were dying to get past him.

"Meet me at midnight in the science lab and I'll tell you."

I laughed. "Yeah, right. First of all, you'd have to have the key to get in."

He waved the key in my face.

"And second, I don't even know you. You think I'm going to meet you in the middle of the night? In some dark, empty classroom? So not going to happen."

"That's up to you, of course. But I do have the answers to those questions you've been asking yourself."

"I don't have any questions."

"Sure you do. Those deep questions, like," he paused for maximum dramatic effect, "is there life after high school?"

I rolled my eyes. "Please."

"Is life about choice or destiny? Or no, no, how about, 'Who am I really?' All those deep teenage questions: Am I what I think or am I what other people think I am? Let's walk through the looking glass and find out."

"This is all utterly precious but I have to—"

He held my arm and turned serious on me. "I really do have something I need to tell you."

I punched his arm and he let go with a cringe. "You touch me again and I'll flatten you."

"Please meet me tonight? It's important." He shook the arm I punched. "God, girls are so violent." He walked around the corner.

I knew I wouldn't go, and went to the corner to say so, but he was gone. I thought maybe he'd ducked into the first class, but I doubted it—that was some Home Economics class. How did he disappear like that? Was he really my Fairy Godfather?

"Who are you talking to?"

I thought my heart was going to detonate. It took all my effort not to turn around and punch Patty for scaring me. "Damn it, Patty! Why do you do that shit?"

"What shit?"

"You're always sneaking up on me and scaring me!"

"I am? Sorry, I didn't realize."

I exhaled slowly to clear my head. "What happened, did you hear?"

"Well, I guess Renee started a protest—"

"I know about that. I mean is Monroe going to suspend her?"

"Oh. Yeah, I guess so." Patty said it in an "isn't-it-a-shame" voice, with an "I'm-secretly-loving-it" glint in her eye. I think she liked the idea of Renee for once not getting away with everything. "She probably won't be going out with us tonight."

"Tonight?"

"The drive-in! We're going to see those two scary movies. You know, the one about the pod people and how they grow bodies just like the other people in this town and then they kill the people and pretend to be them, but they're really these aliens and there's these two versions, one's black and white and the other's in color, and we're supposed to go with the guys, remember?"

"Hmm."

"Well, you're going aren't you?"

I shrugged. "If there's nothing better to do." I walked down the hall and Patty followed me, begging the whole way.

* * *

Drive-ins rarely exist anymore, but we have one. It's called the B-52 Drive-In and out front there's an actual replica of a B-52 airplane—a scaled-down size, of course. My friends and I have spent more evenings than I could count flying that plane in a drunken frenzy around the stars of a still black night.

My initials are under the wing. Sort of the right armpit, if a plane could have an arm. I put them there because I wanted a memory, but I didn't want to share it with just anyone who happened by. By that time, I had come to the conclusion that I was quite private about most things.

Patty and I picked up Diane a block from her house with no questions asked as to why there, though we knew it had to do with her parents being strict and she must have lied to them about where she was going. We parked a distance from the drive-in, walked to the wall and waited. Patty had a bottle of Southern Comfort and we all took turns taking a drink. When Diane's turn came, her face distorted into a grimace after a swallow and it made me want to tease her, but I didn't because of how serious she was taking it all.

As dusk fell into the dark pocket of a moonless night, Patty, Diane and I jumped the wall behind the big movie screen—Diane and I because we couldn't afford admission. Patty, though she could have paid, jumped for the thrill. Perhaps if I had money, I might've jumped anyway.

As we passed along the wall, I watched the large faces looming above us like disembodied gods. This place was the most magical place I knew. I sometimes came alone to watch my favorite movies. Sitting in a lawn chair, feeling the dirt beneath my toes, I would watch the large screen under the open sky, the gentle wind touching me, tickling my ears.

We moved quickly to the back row. There, in the middle, was a group of cars and trucks. In a big four-wheel drive Chevy was a keg of beer on ice. All around the truck were lawn chairs and blankets and people drinking beer, laughing and standing real close to each other.

Patty ran off to a car with a bunch of guys in it. I bet it was because Paul Rand was there. Ricky was sitting in the back of a blue truck waving an extra blanket at me. I didn't want to leave Diane alone and was going to ask her to sit with us, but Patty was calling to her. The guys were now standing outside of their car, at least three of them staring moony-eyed at Diane.

She looked at me with a tired desperation. I started to say she didn't have to go but Patty called her again and Diane put on a smile and went off like a well-trained dog. I shook my head. She was way too polite. It would wear her too thin some day.

The body snatchers were interesting, the way they went around stealing people's individuality. That's what I thought anyway, that they were taking away what made people who they were, and turning them instead into robot-like creatures. Ricky said that it was more than that, that the aliens killed the people and that they then took over pretending to be the dead people. I couldn't figure out what the hell the difference was, either way you're dead.

However, it did explain the pods.

The idea of pod people existing explained a good deal about a lot of the people I knew. Just like the pod people, they all walked, talked and acted the same. A chill went down my spine as I imagined my whole high school screaming that high-pitched squeal, twisting their pod faces and pointing at anyone who wasn't one of them.

"Are you cold?" Ricky asked.

I pulled the blanket closer. "A little." In fact, I was pretty warm.

Ricky pulled me down into the bed of the truck and we snuggled, which was fine with me because I had a gut feeling the pod people were going to win and I couldn't bear it.

A voice floated over our heads. "Ella?"

I sat up and saw Diane and saw that she was taken aback. I saw on her face that I shocked her by being under the blanket with Ricky.

"Oh, I'm sorry." She looked away as though she might see some covert sex act.

I chuckled. Her innocence was oddly charming. "Where are you going?"

"They're nice guys but…" She motioned to the group she had been sitting with and intimated she was unhappy.

"Here," I said, opening my blanket and inviting her to sit next to me, "it's nice and warm."

I smoothed the blanket, she looked at the space I held open for her and bit her lower lip. When her eyes met mine she seemed undecided. Her gaze fell on Ricky, who was watching the movie. I tilted my head and made like I was getting impatient. That made her smile and she climbed into the back of the truck. I gave her part of my blanket and let her lean against me. She shivered and I pulled the blanket closer around her shoulders. But as I touched the skin on her arm she seemed as toasty warm as me.

I settled in to watch the movie but her hair, so curly and unruly, was in my way. I freed a hand and meant to move her hair to one side, but as soon as my hand touched her neck she jumped and turned. "I'm sorry. Your hair was in my way…" But the look on her face stopped me. Her eyes were glassy and her lips looked almost swollen. She turned quickly away from my watchful eyes, looking forward, her hair hiding her expression.

I thought I did something wrong. Can you offend someone by touching her hair? I leaned forward, careful not to touch her again, and whispered into her ear, "Sorry."

She hesitated briefly before leaning her head back, resting it on my shoulder and whispering back to me, "No, don't be. I'm sorry."

Well, I had no idea what she was sorry about. And she didn't move, but stayed there, leaning against me. Her hair curled around my face, tickling my nose and my lips.

Diane put her hand on my knee and I responded, I swear like it was instinct, and put my arm around her back. She pulled my arm up under her arm and laced her fingers with mine. She scooted back just slightly and filled the crook of my arm with her body. My cheek was nearly resting on her cheek.

I cut my eyes toward Ricky. I wondered if he noticed that I was no longer cuddling with him but with Diane instead. But he was paying no attention, watching the movie and talking with some guy I didn't know.

I have always been affectionate with my friends, but I knew this was different. And for some reason, every second that passed felt like I was getting away with some forbidden pleasure, some long-awaited decadence. Diane was luxurious, and a thrill shot through me as I leaned closer.

We stayed that way even though my butt was falling asleep, and I'm sure she must have been uncomfortable too. People walked by, said hi and tried to get us to go to the snack bar and the bathroom at intermission, but I knew we had conspired not to move. No one could see we were holding hands and stuff. It just looked like we were keeping warm.

The second movie was halfway through but I wasn't following it too much—if you've seen one pod story, you've seen them all—and instead I found myself listening to Diane's breathing, shallow and quicker than before. I turned my nose into her hair and inhaled her scent. When she startled and looked at me, I faced forward, pretending to be extremely engrossed in the movie.

A car came driving down the aisle behind us. I didn't pay much attention until I heard footsteps stopping beside the truck. When I looked up, Renee was standing there. And how she looked at us was different than how anyone else had. There was something hurt and accusing in her face, but even worse, there was a defeated look and it made me jerk my hand from Diane's. I felt guilty, though I couldn't say why exactly, then

I had a flashback to when I was in the third grade and how upset Bethie Myers had been when I started playing at Sarah O'Connell's house. Damn. It just sucked.

"I thought you were grounded," I said.

"Altman snuck me out."

"Oh…that's cool."

No one said anything else. Renee kept looking at us.

"Do you want to sit down? We have enough blankets." Diane offered.

It relieved me when she asked Renee that. It would prove that Diane and I weren't out to be new playmates that would close her out, play jump rope and dolls without asking her to join. Though part of me wondered if that wasn't exactly what I wanted, and why I felt guilty.

I also hoped it meant that Diane wasn't mad at me for pulling away from her.

"No, I just came to tell you we're heading over to the Taco Stand if you want to come," Renee said, directing the invitation to me. "You too, Lacey, if you want to party."

"Maybe after the movie," I said. My awkwardness felt icky.

Renee nodded and looked at Diane with a questioning eyebrow.

"I don't think so," Diane said. "Thanks, but I have to go home."

"Well, I guess I'll see you when I see you," Renee said to me. She looked at Diane then back at me. "Enjoy the movie."

She walked back to the car and she and Altman drove out of the drive-in, dirt flying up behind them.

Diane turned to me. "You know, if you want to go now, I can find a ride—"

"I don't want to go." I knew my response was too abrupt.

Diane turned toward the screen and wrapped her arms around her knees. She wouldn't lean back, and she wouldn't touch me anymore.

I knew this time I had really offended her, but I just couldn't do anything about it. I felt too confused.

* * *

When I dropped Patty and Diane off, I made sure to take Diane home first. The less I had to talk, or look at her, the sooner I would feel normal again. Still, when she got out of the car, I looked at her out of politeness. Her face held me hostage. Something about it seemed to change from the face I used to know. It was as if, for this split second, I could suddenly see how things really were, how she really felt—this need in her eyes that scared me. I could see beneath her skin, how her bones were like her needs, these fragile, delicate things that barely held her together. They were paper-thin, bleached-white, bones that would shatter too easily.

I was careful not to squeal away from the curb leaving Diane in my wake, but I wanted so badly to get away. My hands shook on the steering wheel.

After dropping off Patty, I was on my way to the Taco Stand, though my plan was to only stay a minute, but on my way there I passed by the high school and remembered that guy—my Fairy Godfather, yeah right—asking me to meet him. I looked at my watch. It was nearly midnight. I chuckled a little. The coincidence intrigued me, so I pulled into the parking lot and, honestly, it was pretty fucking spooky.

Like all Southern California schools, the classrooms weren't enclosed in a building, so I just made my way through the night along the hallways and the various structures to the science classroom. When I tried the doorknob, it turned. I pushed open the door and the creak of it echoed. It was dark inside the room and the air was heavy in the blackness. It struck me this was really dumb because he surely wasn't going to be there. I let the weight of the door rest against me, feeling more comfortable with access to a quick exit.

"Hello?" I squeaked, sounding like a frightened little mouse. That was annoying.

A moment of nerves blanketed me and I was ready to turn and leave, shake my head at my silly fears, and beat it the hell out of there. But there was a click and light appeared from across the room.

He delivered the old joke, a flashlight under the chin. His mischievous lips held a lit cigarette, smoke and light playing against the planes of his face. "Drama, drama, drama. I like it. It's fun." The light flicked off and his laughter was deep and amused.

He'd startled me, but I didn't want him to know it. "I'm turning the light on."

"What for, Cinderella? To look your destiny in the eye?"

"What?" I was in a game of cat and mouse.

He laughed and turned on a dim electric lantern of some sort. "If you turn on the room lights someone might notice." He was sitting at the end of one of those long tables they always seem to have in the science rooms. "I wasn't sure you'd show up. Have a seat." He gestured to a stool a few feet away from him.

I hesitated briefly before stepping into the classroom. The door, made thick and heavy, closed with the finality of a tomb. It made me wonder what I was doing. How did I know that he wasn't some kind of crazed serial murderer? No one knew anything about his background.

The coldness of the room grabbed me by the back of the neck and I was sure I could smell dead frogs.

He didn't seem to notice, or care, about my discomfort.

I didn't say anything because I wanted to force his conversation. But he said no more and watched me patiently. I noticed that safety pins seemed to hold much of his clothing together. He was definitely a punk, so at least we had that in common.

"So, I'm waiting? Why am I here? Where are those answers you promised to all my questions?" I asked.

His patience showed in his smile. "I kind of baited you when I said that."

"Why?" The idea of being lured here made me uneasy.

"Because I'm your Fairy Godfather. I'm here to help you, but you don't think you need any help. The truth is that only you have the answers to those questions. Is your life fated to follow the old story? Or are you ready to forge a new story, one that belongs solely to you?"

"Okay, clearly you know my full name is Cinderella. I get it. Look, I've dealt with this my whole life. So, if you think this is some fun game to come in and play with me this way, get real. It's old. I've heard it a million times. You're not cute, or original, it's just boring."

"I know it's been hard, but I am who I say I am."

"You honestly think you're my Fairy Godfather? Okay, do something magical. Sprout fairy wings. Fly around the room. Sprinkle fairy dust on this Petri dish and turn it into a Trans Am. Do something to make me believe in you."

He stared at me a bit too long. It made me uneasy. Maybe I'd just pissed off a crazy person.

"Everyone has a story, Cinderella. You just happen to have a very famous one. Most people are trying to live their life by these stories, but they will never really succeed. You see, they are just guideposts, they aren't meant to be taken literally."

I understood the concept of what he was saying—after all, I took English, I understood metaphor and parables, and the general thrust of the traditional fairy tales.

"But it's a little difficult to accept this premise when your mother left you because, to her, they were real. So you became anything but the princess. In fact, you chose the opposite. You became the Knight. At least, as the Knight, you are closer to the truth. But it's still not the whole truth. And it's still not your full story. You have yet to discover that, much less start telling it and living it. But you're getting closer. Don't you feel it? It's all changing. The story you thought was yours has suddenly veered off the narrative and you are finding yourself suddenly in this new story. You're looking around and realizing that you don't know where you are, you've never seen this place before. And all the characters are changing. It is some story you didn't even know existed. And it's not going to stop. In fact, it's going to start moving faster and faster and before you know it you are going to be so deep in this other story that you'll feel like you're drowning. But it doesn't have to be that way. It's only that way because you won't acknowledge it—won't acknowledge the story is changing because you're holding on so tightly to the old story, the one you've outgrown. But if you continue that way, if you don't acknowledge and accept the new story, it will take you down. It won't end the way it should. It will be a tragedy, a cautionary tale. But if you are willing to go with the change, accept it, and even help to create it and narrate it, you will have your happy ending. Well, at least until a new story is ready to be told. So, how's that? Was that magical enough?"

I couldn't breathe. I was filled with fear that I didn't completely understand. How did he know so much about me? It was a small town and most people knew something about me, at least that my mom left. I knew people talked, and I had some problems when I was young with kids who knew the story, but I thought most of that was behind me. And this guy was new. Who did he pump for this information? I felt claustrophobic. I needed to get out of that room. "I have to go."

"Wait," he said. "Tell me, do you believe in me? Believe in me enough to let me help you?"

"I don't know what I believe." I stepped down from the stool and stumbled. I backed up, keeping distance between us, and walked to the door. He didn't try to stop me.

"Well, what about love? Do you believe in love? True love? The type dreams are made of? What do you believe in, Cinderella?" He pulled on the safety pin dangling from his right ear.

Did I? What did I believe in? I huffed in frustration. "I don't know what you want from me."

"To know that pretty soon you won't recognize yourself. You'll feel like a mythical being, the types you've heard about in fairy tales: unicorns, elves, sprites. You'll begin to question who you are because you've never seen another of your kind in this human world, so you won't believe you're real."

"You mean like a fairy godfather isn't real?" I said with a bite.

"But you are real, my little unicorn. The question is: what do you want from your story? It's time to ponder these questions. Because the story is on the march, it's moving forward with or without you. Time to decide. The clock is ticking. Ticktock, ticktock…"

I searched my brain for something to say to him, but my mind wasn't cooperating. I made some noise of frustration and swung the door open wide and walked out.

I ran down the dark corridor. The echo of my feet hitting the pavement in the darkness was spooking me. That's when I heard the Cinderella song—"A Dream is a Wish Your Heart Makes." Low, not too loud. I recognized it immediately. My mother used to play it every day.

I was so frightened I felt as if I was choking, like the words of the song were wrapping around my throat. I ran faster and faster, until I was at my top speed, running as fast as I could to get away from the music.

CHAPTER NINE

So Goddamn Pure

Near the end of every spring, for the last four years, we took a trip to Patty's beach house. It's always our first trip of the warm season.

Friendships and boyfriends come and go but Patty, Renee and I have been there every year. This year we invited Diane.

We were driving down in the spare car from Patty's house, a Cadillac with five years off its life. It was considered the "expendable car" and so we were allowed to use it. The backseat was more comfortable than my couch at home. It was at times like this when I realized Patty's experience of life was quite different from mine. Yet Patty never seemed to notice our lumpy couches, or the rough ride of our old Volkswagens, any more than she noticed the luxury of the cruise control in her parents' Cadillac.

The radio station we were listening to was having an A to Z rock 'n' roll weekend. We had picked up with The Babys' "Isn't It Time" and were currently listening to J. Geils' "One Last Kiss." We were drinking beer from a twelve-pack we spotted at Cactus Liquor before we headed out of town. To "spot some beer" was to get someone of legal age to buy the alcohol for you. Patty was the best at spotting because she looked like an upstanding citizen and old enough to party, so older guys would often buy booze for her. Renee intimidated people and I don't think anyone took me seriously—I looked like some punk street kid. Diane was too sweet and innocent with no street smarts at all since she had been locked away in a "tower" her whole life.

The sun had set during our drive, and most of the beer was gone. Patty and Renee were in the front seat. Patty was driving and keeping beat with her hands on the steering wheel. Renee, with her feet up on the dash, was singing along with Patty, obnoxiously loud most of the time. I sat behind Patty, my legs crossed Indian style, singing softly, feeling mellower than Renee and Patty. I was hoping for a long J. Geils' set, hoping that maybe they would play "Sanctuary." I smiled at Diane, who was sitting next to me. She was kicking back like me, practically glowing when she returned my smile. I felt a pang of sadness that her good times were just beginning, and here it was so near the end.

We were merging into heavier traffic when Patty started flirting with a truckload of guys. Two were in front, and two were in the bed of an old clunker of a truck.

"Where you headed?" the passenger screamed.

"Mexico!" Patty lied.

"We'll escort you!" yelled one of the guys in the back.

Renee leaned over Patty and shouted. "Don't need an escort!"

"Come on, pull over and we'll have a party!"

Patty threw her head back and laughed.

"Eat your heart out, baby!" And Renee, in one swift move, pulled her shirt over her head to expose naked, bouncing breasts.

The guys in the truck yelled and hooted. Patty, howling with laughter, made Renee take the wheel as she pulled her shirt off too.

Diane and I gawked at each other. She grabbed for the bottom of her shirt, and I reached down for mine, and on the count of three we both pulled our shirts over our heads. None of us had bras on and we shook all that we had out the windows.

The boys were nearly hanging out of the truck and gesturing wildly for us to pull over. As we whooped and swung our shirts over our heads, Patty hit the accelerator and threw our nipples to the wind, leaving the boys and their clunker truck in titty heaven.

I was nearly off the seat and on the floor of the car, crying with laughter. Renee, still laughing, turned around in her seat to see where the truck was, her naked breasts shoved in my face. I stopped laughing and looked for my shirt.

"Here." Diane handed my shirt to me.

I thanked her and put it on. I looked at Diane again just as she was looking away. I could have sworn she was looking at my breasts. My eyes wandered down to the tank top she had already put back on. God, I felt suddenly sober. I made a joke about the guys in the truck and Diane smiled but kept looking out the window. Patty and Renee, feeling proud, pushed their chests out and proclaimed freedom, making the decision to drive the rest of the way with their shirts off.

We were almost to the beach house, but after that the drive seemed to take for-fucking-ever.

When we arrived, Patty and Renee finally put their shirts back on, mercifully, because we found Altman, Gerrard Daniels and Chad Walker there. They had built a fire on the beach. We didn't know they were there at first because people were always building campfires on the beach. Patty had figured it was the neighbors, who were about an acre away on either side. But as we were carrying our bags into the house, Altman appeared out of nowhere. He grabbed Renee, picked her up and spun her around.

"Put me down!" Renee yelled, livid as all hell.

Altman laughed and spun her around again.

"I said, put me down, goddamn it!"

He put her down but continued to embrace her. I could barely make out her muffled curses against his chest.

"We came down to surprise you!" Altman said, grinning big as he grabbed her by the face and kissed her sloppily on her forehead and cheeks, then a big smack on the lips that Renee emerged from gasping for air.

"Jesus Christ!" She pushed his massive chest away from her. "You trying to kill me? Jesus!" She shook her head and picked up her bags, walking into the house mumbling.

Altman stood with his hands on his hips and laughed, looking a little like Yul Brynner in the "King and I" and that sort of made me laugh.

"You guys knew this was supposed to be girls only," Patty said looking past Altman at Gerrard.

I bet she wouldn't have said that if Gerrard had been Paul Rand. She probably would have thrown roses in the doorway and done an interpretive dance of welcome.

"Hi Diane." Chad was sitting on the porch rail, his shirt off. He was twisting it over and over again to show off his arm muscles.

"Hi." With a flip of her wrist, Diane threw her hair over her shoulder and walked past him into the house.

Patty followed after her.

I looked at the three guys. "Well, you're here. I guess you might as well come in."

* * *

"I'll kick your ass!"

"No, fucking way! I've never been beat at this game!"

"You're beat now!"

"Beat this, fag boy!"

"Are we going to play, or not?" I was getting pretty bored with Altman and Chad's competitive banter. We had been playing drinking games for the past few hours, during which we had all endured this idiotic crap. Gerrard grinned stupidly, drunk as a mouse on a thimble of beer. He tried to grab Patty every time she walked by.

The place was cozy, with a fireplace and fluffy armchairs and an eight-foot foldout couch. The art on the wall was completely generic—basically pictures of other beach houses from other parts of the country. (I mean, seriously, if you're already at a beach house, would you want to see pictures of other beach houses?). There were two bedrooms and a well-stocked kitchen. The stereo system left a lot to be desired, nothing but an old eight-track player. Someone had put in a Boz Scaggs cassette. "It's Over" was playing and it was sad and beautiful and extremely corny, but since I was also extremely buzzed it made me feel all gooey and sentimental.

Patty and Diane were playing cards by the fire, having long ago abandoned our drinking games. They sipped rum and Coke and quietly played gin rummy. I was the only girl still playing. Renee had gone for a walk.

We were all smoking cigars and playing for shots of beer. I chewed on my stogy and watched Gerrard's forehead bang hard on the table as he passed out. Altman bounced the quarter and missed. Chad laughed in his face and snatched up the coin. It made it into the shot glass and he pointed his elbow at me. "Consume!"

I drained my glass and picked up the quarter. "If I can make this five times in a row you each have to…" I paused to think of something good because I was in a real gambling mood. They thought I was pausing for effect. "You have to," their eyes went wild with the possibilities, "take off your clothes…"

Chad hooted loudly.

"…go to the houses next door…"

"What?" Altman cried.

"…and tell them you're on a scavenger hunt…"

Patty and Diane laughed.

"…tell them you're looking for a pair of women's underwear."

Patty and Diane were rolling.

"You're crazy!" Altman said.

"Look, what are the chances I'll make five out of five?" I asked, gesturing widely and letting my cigar bob up and down as I talked.

He looked at Chad. "No way," Chad said, "she'll never do it."

"Okay, deal," Altman said.

I took the quarter without hesitation and easily made the first one.

"Luck," Chad said.

I made the next three so quickly they didn't have time to comment. The last one I made with flair, flicking my wrist at the end, just like I always do when I practice at home. Patty laughed, knowing the whole time I would make all five.

"No way!" Chad said and shook his head.

"A bet's a bet. You can't renege. You agreed." I turned to Patty and Diane. "Didn't he?" They both nodded, smiling mischievously.

"Come on," Altman said, punching Chad in the arm.

"The deal is you have to come back with the underwear," I said.

"No, the deal is, we'll try and get it. You know there's no way we will!" Altman argued.

"How will we know if you did it unless you bring something back?" I asked.

Altman put his hand on my leg, under the table where no one could see. "You could come with us and watch."

I brushed his hand away. "No. Think of another way."

Chad turned to Diane. "Why don't you come with us?"

Diane looked away pretending not to hear him.

Altman stood up. "We'll figure out a way to prove it, come on."

As they got up to leave, Chad went over and tried to take Diane by the hand. He mumbled something to her that no one else could hear. She pulled away from him and Altman yanked him away by the collar. Was Altman being protective of Diane? Unlikely. More likely that because he didn't get what he wanted, he was going to make sure Chad didn't either. Altman was the type to orchestrate things—he liked power. I think that's why he was with Renee. She had power and he sucked it from her like a leech. I think part of him also hated her for having that power. He wanted to break her.

I walked out onto the porch and watched them run off down the beach until I couldn't see them anymore. Diane stood next to me.

"What made you think of that?" she asked.

"They were getting on my nerves. I didn't actually think they'd do it."

"Want to take a walk?"

We went the opposite way so we wouldn't run into Chad or Altman naked. There was very little moon, so we walked slowly along the edge of the water, seeing only a short distance ahead of us. I kept turning to keep sight of the lights from the beach house.

The breeze was cool and damp on my face. I had a hard time walking, so I put my arm around Diane's neck for balance. She steadied me, but I tried not to lean too heavily on her.

"What cute hair!" I fingered her curls, which were even curlier because of the humidity in the air.

"Thank you. You have cute hair too."

"No! Really? I think you're humoring me."

She laughed. "I think you're drunk."

"I am. I'm drunk. I admit it."

"Look." She pointed, but I had no idea at what. I couldn't see a thing. "Let's sit down."

She led me to a small enclosure and we sat down in the soft sand. Our back and sides were surrounded by rock, protecting us most of the time from wind, but it was blowing in unpredictable gusts.

I could hear the waves lapping against the shore as I watched Diane siphon sand through her fingers. I watched her, imagining the feeling of graininess falling into the pit of my stomach. It was having a relaxing effect on me.

She set down a bottle of wine between us and we drank from it. Good wine, it came from Patty's parents' wine cellar, and we drank it straight from the bottle.

"Renee's out here somewhere," I said, remembering she had left for a walk. I wondered if she was okay.

"She most certainly is," Diane said in a really odd way.

"What?" I asked. I tried to understand the hidden meaning that I knew was there.

"Nothing."

"So what do you think of the beach house?"

"It's nice. I was hoping for more privacy, but it's better than being at home."

"Yeah, you really didn't get to do much until this year. Are the guys really annoying you? None of us will let Chad, you know, bother you."

She smiled and chuckled in an amused way, like there was something funny that I wouldn't understand. "Sure, I know that."

"What's so funny?"

"Nothing."

"Really, I want to know."

"It's nothing, honestly."

"Look, I know *something* when I hear *something*! So, what is it?"

"You wouldn't believe me if I told you."

"Sure I would."

"No, I don't think so."

I looked at her, exasperated as all hell. "Why the heck wouldn't I?"

She leaned over and kissed me on the mouth. It was the softest kiss I ever felt, so soft, I wasn't sure it really happened.

I was paralyzed.

She was still leaning close to me. I saw her lips tremble. "I told you."

A million things came to my mind, like a million years worth of knowledge, but none of it would take cohesive form.

The booze and Diane's kiss numbed my brain, I felt woozy. My head was drowning in surrealistic images. I saw her coming closer to me. I saw her lips part. And when I saw that, that simple opening of her mouth, it was the most complex, profound moment of my life. There was not a single cell in my body that remained indifferent to that small, effortless movement. Then I heard Altman call my name. Diane pulled back, startled, and stood up. That's when I realized I wasn't hallucinating Altman's deep voice.

"There you are! Look here!" A pair of women's underwear fell into my lap. I held up the underwear and laughed. I didn't want to laugh, but it somehow seemed like the only thing left to do.

The alcohol we just drank hit me hard and I fell on my side, into the sand. When I did, the wind picked up, throwing sand in my face, into my mouth. I tried to spit it out but it seemed like it was glued there. When I looked up Altman was standing there in his bathing trunks.

"Where's Diane?" I asked.

"She ran off just as I walked up. Are you two fighting?"

Realizing the irony, I found that quite funny and I laughed again. "No, definitely not fighting."

"What happened?" Altman asked. He was so nosy, always had been. I don't know why they say women are that way because he's the absolute worst.

"Nothing happened." I saw her lips parting. "Nothing happened," I repeated.

"Okay, nothing happened." He put his hand on my leg and moved closer to me. I thought about the feel of her lips, the light pressure. He kissed me and I could feel the roughness of his face. He pushed me back onto the sand and lay on top of me. My mind jammed in a loop: the barely recognizable kiss, then her parting lips, the kiss and the parting lips. He had my shirt unbuttoned and I felt him pulling off my shorts. The kiss, and then she parted her lips, and then I realized—*she was going to kiss me again.* He spread my legs. I think I passed out because I heard a bang, like someone was banging on a door. I panicked. It was Altman, he was breaking down the door.

Everything fell away again and all I could think was *How could she make me feel that way?* And here was Altman, easily the best looking guy in school and I felt nothing. His body left me cold. The truth? So did Ricky, as much as I cared for him. But that one small kiss from Diane was an earthquake through my body. What the hell was wrong with me?

He tried and tried but I was locked and closed to him. I couldn't relax and it started to hurt. I heard myself say no. I pushed him away. I thought our bodies had minds of their own. His wanted in me. Mine wanted him out. I almost laughed out loud before I choked back a sob.

I told him he was too big. This, his ego could handle, he could understand, and so he stopped. Everything was swirling around me. I saw his face and thought of Renee. I rolled on my side and vomited on a rock.

* * *

Back at the porch, Altman tried to kiss me but I pulled away. I was hostile.

"Look," he said, "I don't want you to feel like this. I really like you."

"Get the fuck away from me."

"I don't want to leave you alone."

"Leave me alone. Really. Trust me. I want to be alone."

He went past me into the house. I tried to walk but I stumbled and wasn't sure I would make it any farther without someone's help.

In the shadows, I saw movement. It was then that I realized I always saw movement in the shadows, like there was something out there just waiting to get me, and out of the dark came Diane. She had a blanket wrapped around her. Like some saint was how she looked—always so goddamn pure.

I held onto the porch railing for balance. As she came closer her face appeared hard like a china plate. I almost cried. I think I whispered, *I'm sorry*. She looked down at my clothes. I followed her gaze and saw how disheveled I was—shirt untucked and, worst of all, buttoned wrong. Shame washed over me. I tried to button myself up properly, but I fumbled, my hands shaking.

Diane reached out, letting her blanket fall to the ground, and started unbuttoning my shirt. Underneath I wore nothing, my discarded bra having been tucked into my shorts, and her fingers lightly grazed the skin on my stomach and my breasts as she undid the last button. I looked up into her golden eyes. She held my gaze briefly, then looked back down and buttoned my shirt correctly.

When she hooked the last button, she looked up at me, and was so close that I thought she might kiss me again. I thought it would be just so light, almost motherly except that her eyes would be wild. That's when I realized I was holding my breath. I became unbearably self-conscious. I was drunk and had vomit on my breath. I understood in absolute terms that my heart was beating fast because of her.

She picked up the blanket and wrapped it around me, pulling it close like a mother would do for a child on a rainy day, except no mother's eyes would burn through me like hers did.

She backed away from me until she reached the edge of the porch. She looked at me over her shoulder before she disappeared into the blackness.

My life had become filled with shadows—apparitions coming and going through corridors of black clouds. Soot with light.

* * *

I came to with a soft bed beneath me. Renee was standing over me and soft light was coming from somewhere beyond her. Her hair fell over me, gold with light—angel hair. I thought maybe Renee was an angel and I had died, because everything seemed tranquil and perfectly still.

She kissed my forehead and sailed upward. I thought she was going to heaven without me. I wrapped my arms around her neck, thinking she would take me with her.

I waited for our bodies to become weightless and Renee laughed into my ear, "What is it, my Cinderella?" She told me, in a reassuring voice, "I won't leave you." I relaxed my hold on her and she did stay. I could feel her close, breathing on my neck.

Things dulled and went dark but not before I could recall Renee's fingers lacing together with mine.

* * *

Noise awoke me from the dark pit of unconsciousness. A bang. I opened my eyes and saw a door closing.

It took me a while to figure out where I was, but when I turned over I saw Renee lying beside me and I recognized the decor of the bedroom, remembering I was at Patty's beach house. A cyclone of memories whirled about my head in quick procession like a roller coaster. The physical reaction was astonishing, and I literally had to hold my stomach to keep it from leaving my body and flying away.

The room blurred and I let my eyes close.

When I woke up again, it was dread that lay next to me. Renee had already gotten up. I could hear voices in the house, lively and awake. My head was pounding and I stayed as long as I could in the bedroom looking at a scuff on the wall. I wasted as much time as I could trying to figure out how it happened. Did I mean the scuff on the wall, or everything else from last night? What difference would it make? It was all so hopeless.

* * *

"It's about time you got up, lazy bones," Chad said to me. He was in the kitchen with Altman. They were fixing breakfast. I could smell the bacon.

I'd already gone to the bathroom and showered. I gargled twice but I still felt as though something died in my mouth. I sat down at the kitchen table and held my head in my hands. I had a roaring headache.

"Hangovers. One of life's little lessons," Renee said.

She was feeling fine since she rarely drank much. She was sitting across from me. I looked at her expecting anything besides the genuine look of concern in her eyes. Flashbacks of the evening pushed at me, but I pushed back.

When I didn't say anything she went back to her sketching. I wondered where she was last night and what she had done. Maybe she was into black magic and animal sacrifice, offering furry animals up to a moon-filled sky.

I knew I was just feeling guilty and shitty.

The screen door slammed and Patty and Paul Rand came in. He went into the kitchen and Patty sat at the table with us.

"When did he get here?" I asked.

"A few hours ago." Patty sat down and picked up a charred piece of bacon.

"That's why Gerrard left," Renee said.

Patty shrugged to indicate she didn't care one way or another what Gerrard did. "I wonder why Diane left with him. I bet it's because of Chad."

"Could be." Renee looked at me.

I mean she looked at me like she just knew it had to do with me.

I couldn't believe that Diane left. I felt relief mixed with a deep down-to-the-bones sadness, but this newest development did allow me to relax, and I leaned back in my chair and looked around.

From the kitchen, Altman was looking at me with a secretive smile on his lips. I understood it all in that split second. Part of his addiction to cheating was the secret, the forbidden connection. And the control. Christ, the massive amount of control he now had was mind-boggling. It was pure genius. It sickened me and I ignored him. If he was looking for some forbidden connection, some secret thrill, I'd make sure he never got his fix.

I also lost my fleeting moment of respite.

* * *

At any given chance, I would go off by myself. There were places to hide out along the beach and I would take a towel, a soda, and fall asleep. When I couldn't sleep, I thought about that night. I thought about it to the point that it became *That Night*. I started to see how things could become more important and bigger with each recollection. Knowing that, I did my best not to relive it too much.

I watched the sun bake the rocks near the shore until the tide came in, breaking a cool wave on their surface, then the sun would warm the black-gray rocks again.

I began to think of myself as special. I thought I was different and unique, which brought on fits of self-pity and, at other times, grand ideas of superiority. I was certainly more evolved and greater than my friends—they could never truly understand my complexity. Then I would tailspin again into despair over what happened. I felt worthless and despicable. Nothing could change what I had actually done with Altman, and it would most certainly be judged alone—a subject without a background. I was doomed.

What had occurred with Altman brought on the pain. It had concrete repercussions. Diane brought on more of a haze, a precursor for what had happened later with Altman. Thinking about the kiss with Diane was a direct line to the later incident, so I couldn't examine it independently. Though it was that point that would first intrigue me, draw me into the memory, fuzzy as it was. I might have been able to stuff down the other memory if it weren't for that kiss with Diane. It was a spark I couldn't stop looking at.

I turned on my back and tried to let the sun lull me into a trance. I was just beginning to let go when I felt a cool shadow move across me. I was instantly bothered and wondered why I couldn't be left alone. When I opened my eyes, I saw Ricky. He was smiling, pleased with himself over his surprise. I have never been so glad to see anyone.

He sat down next to me and I sat up and hugged him. He held on to me when I fell apart in his arms, crying into his chest. I cried over everything that had happened. I cried over all my analyzing of what had happened, that it had happened to me, and that I couldn't change it.

When I stopped crying, I sat still and listened to Ricky's heart. He was my friend, in a deep-rooted way that was not balanced on conditions. I knew it was a secondary love, but somehow the most exceptional love, because it couldn't be beat up or tarnished.

He never asked me what was wrong. He just held me until he didn't need to anymore. It was exactly right, and exactly what a secondary love should do.

CHAPTER TEN

The Farmer's Daughter

At school I found myself avoiding Renee and Diane. I knew their classes and the routes they followed and I avoided them. It was harder to avoid Renee because when I wasn't around she looked for me, and we always had planned parts of the day when we were supposed to meet.

My third and last class of the day was government. Renee still had a history class to attend, so we always met and had a Coke before I went home and she went on to her history class. It was the one time of the day that I knew I'd see Renee, no matter what.

When we were alone on these occasions, I found them tolerable. I could forget everything except Renee and that moment. It was when Altman barged in that things became a masquerade and everything seemed so ugly. He would throw his arm around Renee and wink at me.

"You have something in your eye?" I asked, the acid of my tone bleeding into the words.

Renee looked up at him and Altman, the big liar, would poke and rub his eye as though something were really there.

"I have things to do at home," I told Renee.

It only got worse. Altman stumbled upon our meetings more and more. Planned stumbling, I'd say. He continued to smile and wink at me as though we had a secret rendezvous planned for every night. I began to believe it wasn't so much that he wanted to feel he was getting away with something—though I didn't rule that out as partly the motive—but that he wanted to claim Renee as his property. And I was the one person he considered a competitor. It was sincerely disgusting to me because I couldn't get the picture of a dog peeing on a tree out of my mind. If he could get away with it, would he pee on her to mark his territory?

I was not a guy so Altman couldn't have challenged me to a fight. So instead he pulled off the one maneuver that could successfully push me from Renee: my betrayal of her. It became more and more plausible that he consciously planned and carried out my betrayal of Renee. By nearly having sex with me, he shut me up for fear I would hang myself as well. It accomplished too many things: my silence about *That Night*; my silence about any other suspicions I had about Altman—granting him greater fucking power; and my secession from Renee—he was making sure of that. I was no longer to be her best friend. He was to be that, or maybe she was not to have a friend at all. And my guilt, my shame regarding what had happened *That Night* made me an accomplice to my own enemy.

The terrible, unexpected thing that grew out of this was my loss of respect for Renee. I tried to fight it, but every time I saw her allowing Altman to determine her life with his manipulations, I was sickened. Like the way he needed her to help him study even though he knew Renee was neglecting her own schoolwork. The way they went to the movies that he wanted to see because the ones Renee wanted to go to were stupid, or women's movies. He changed the station to his music because Renee's music was wimpy and whiny. But most unthinkable was his transgression of her art. More and more, I heard him ask Renee what was more important: her art, which was only a hobby, or their relationship? The progression of his dominance, and her lack of response to it, was mind-boggling. I was unable to control my growing contempt for them both.

I began avoiding them altogether. I would see her standing at the end of the hall looking for me. Her face closed to expression, but her eyes vulnerable and querying. Me standing alongside the lockers, hiding my body from her sight and tasting the bile in my throat. Altman would meet her and I'd watch her search the corridors for me one last time before letting Altman lead her away. Each time I would have to fight back angry, bitter tears.

* * *

It was easier to avoid Diane because she seemed to be avoiding me. About a week after the beach house, I saw her in the hallway and there he was, my supposed Fairy Godfather, standing directly behind her. When he saw me, he smiled and put his arm around Diane. She didn't seem to notice. It's like he wasn't there. I experienced a free-falling sensation in the pit of my stomach and had to lean against a pole for balance. To the unsuspecting eye the scene was innocent enough—casual, friendly, certainly benign—but to my eyes they seemed like a team that could not be beaten if they were to join forces.

Their coupling unnerved me and welded my feet to the pavement. So when Diane, without intent, happened to glance my way, her face showing surprise, I could not move. My Fairy Godfather, seeing her distress, looked and his face grew rigid. His often jester-like eyes were hard and it seemed as though nothing could penetrate something so dark. Did he now belong to her? Had I so completely failed that he'd abandoned me?

His eyes freed my feet and I ran from there as quickly as my shaky legs could carry me. As I ran down the hall, I was scooped up and taken from the hallway.

It was Frances Riley who held me. But I found out her name later. At the time, I only knew her as the Farmer's Daughter. Most people I knew referred to her that way as a sort of crude joke because she was tall and fair and looked hardy, like she came from a farm. In truth, she was the daughter of a rancher.

I once saw her driving her father's old beat-up truck around town when she was about thirteen. I was standing in front of the grocery store with Cherish, my best friend at the time. We were eating candy we had just bought and couldn't wait until we got home to eat. So there we were, being thirteen-year-old kids, eating candy, walking everywhere we went, and here comes this girl, a kid no different than us, *driving a truck.*

She parked right in front of us. She didn't have to. There were plenty of parking spaces available where she could have parked and avoided being seen by us. But no, she pulled up right there on purpose. In the truck, on the passenger side, was a passed out middle-aged man, who we later realized was her father. The girl, gangly and awkwardly skirting puberty like the rest of us, sauntered right past us with a defiant glance. Ten minutes later she exited with her groceries, climbed into the truck and pulled away as if she were an adult housewife doing her shopping for the day. The girl we knew as the Farmer's Daughter held her chin up as though she were the proudest person alive and vaguely smirked at us.

Covertly, among the students, she became an instant legend at our junior high school. The rumor mill had it that because her father was a drunk, she ran the house and took care of her younger brother. She grocery shopped, cooked and drove her brother and herself to and from school every day. If anyone would have cared to pay attention, in the junior high parking lot there was always an old beat-up truck parked at the farthest point away from the school. The unimaginable truth? Not one adult ever noticed. And the kids that knew? Not one ever ratted her out. We let her live. We chose to let her survive.

Now, here was Frances Riley, the legendary driving girl, the Farmer's Daughter, standing in front of me. She asked me what was wrong. With big blue eyes and cheeks—I'm serious, as fair as dove wings, honestly—she didn't look like she belonged in the real world. She was grown up and an Amazon woman if ever there was one. Her fine chestnut hair danced on a slight breeze. She was taller than me, and I had to crane my neck to look at her. And though I had known her for years, meaning I knew *of* her, I didn't know her personally and I had never had such a close look at her. And I most certainly didn't know her well enough to tell her what was wrong. She said I was crying, and to my shock I was, there was wetness all down my cheeks. She took me in her long thin arms and made calming noises and told me it would be all right, like she was soothing one of her father's frightened animals. I knew it was ludicrous, that she couldn't truly tell me any such thing. But I allowed it. Just as I knew I couldn't remain in a busy hallway with tears in my eyes, being comforted by a person I barely knew. Where was my dignity? Yet, I wanted to stay and let Frances tell me everything would be okay. I wanted to believe that my well-being mattered too. So, I allowed it.

* * *

I fell into a surreal existence. What had been my current life became distant, like a far-off city, and a kinder existence replaced it.

I started spending time away from our group, and with other friends who were never actually friends before I saw them as such. With my new friends I became encased, like the girl in the plastic bubble, and I was safe. Nothing could get to me. The other world was a muted blur.

One day Johnny Netti appeared. Like Merlin throwing a pinch of magic dust—poof—he was there. And like Frances, I had known Johnny since we were kids though we never really knew one another. He was easily summed up—which was what teenagers did—by a couple of definitions: guitars and motorcycles. He had a garage band and he was one of the kids in shop. He fixed things and played things. The group he hung out with never crossed paths with mine. Not that we were enemies. We were strangers.

I was standing by the fence in the high school parking lot. I was avoiding everyone and staring, just staring at the railroad tracks and the mountains beyond, thinking about escape, going over the mountains and never coming back when Johnny came up from behind me and said, "I can take you there."

So Johnny Netti took me motorcycle riding out on the local winding roads, out beyond the city limits, through the canyons, around the lakes, up into the mountains. I urged him to go faster, to take the turns tighter. I felt the wind beat my face and the tears stream from the corners of my eyes. I felt the heat from the pavement and fell in love with the bone-breaking certainty of its wrath. Unfailing death as my head would split like a melon on the highway.

I started hanging out with him daily. When we weren't on his bike, he would take me back to his studio where he and his band played music, and he would try to teach me to play the bass guitar. He had dreams of creating the ultimate all-female rock 'n' roll band, one that would challenge greatness, as he didn't believe any truly existed. I tried to tell him about the Runaways, but he didn't know who they were. He was a rock guy through and through—Zeppelin, the Who, the Stones. It was fun to pretend to be a rock 'n' roll girl though, even if I knew it wouldn't be my greatness.

Frances began to come with us out of town. We took her truck—us in the cab and Johnny in the bed of the truck, playing guitar—and drove out into the country where we might find peace, away from the nightmare of our daily lives. What they were running away from, I didn't ask. And they had the decency to not ask me in return. We found a place with a waterfall. We sat and drank beer, smoked weed, and talked about things that didn't have anything to do with school or friends. We weren't meant to be together, we weren't supposed to be. We should have been strangers, but we didn't care. Our trio was misfit and strange and beautiful because of it. We broke the rules, and every second of that freedom was delicious—as if breathing fresh air after a long stay indoors. We didn't discuss it, but I knew they felt the same way.

Our days were simple and devoid of any discussion that didn't involve the present moment. One time we watched a colony of ants all day. They went up and down their little highway of life and we watched their progress. We talked about kitchen ants and how we each witnessed their noxious demise at the end of a Raid can and we wondered if those who killed entire colonies of ants were any better than Hitler. We decided that people who killed ants were mass murderers.

I started cutting classes and going out with Johnny and Frances more and more. Like a snowball rolling downhill, we were out of control. But I couldn't stop it. In the deepest part of me, I felt the trouble mounting, the excuses that would have to be made, outcomes that would have to be accepted because there would be no adequate explanation. But I couldn't stop.

We left in the mornings for the country and wouldn't come back until all other people were in bed. We took guitars and beer and stayed out until the nip in the air became too cold.

Sometimes the only point of going was going.

Johnny Netti would play music almost the whole time. Frances and I sang or sometimes, if it was warm enough, we went swimming in the lake. We'd strip behind a large rock and then take a running leap into the cool water. Johnny sat on the grass, laughing and playing his music louder.

There was this one time when we were really splashing, really meaning it, sending titanic waves at each other, and Frances grabbed my wrists to stop the game. Our faces sopping wet, we laughed hysterically, winding down to a chuckle and a smile, melting into a half-serious look, our eyes met in that way that I was becoming accustomed to, and I'm sure, if Johnny had not been there, something would have happened. My mind goes blank at what, but I am no less sure of the fact.

In school, on TV, and sometimes even our parents were telling us what to do with our lives. How to plan, what to do, how to do it, and whom we should marry. So, in school, I naturally worried about what classes I took and which boys I dated. Now that I was leaving high school, I had no idea what I wanted to do with my life. And even more unexpectedly, I found girls lurking about in the shadows, vying for position, ready to ambush boys. Girls wanted to take the place of boys. A place that girls seemed to believe they deserved, was rightfully theirs. Why had this never been posed as a possibility in life? This should be explained to kids. It wasn't fair to have this type of out-of-the-blue surprise: girls can like girls in this way, fall in love with girls. What kind of secret was this to keep? Was I the only person in the world this was happening to? That couldn't be true because Diane had kissed me. And Frances, well, the way she looked at me felt romantically familiar—that hopeful moment before a kiss. That's when the truth hit me: the world was conspiring to keep this as quiet as possible. This public conspiracy of silence would make everyone believe this type of love didn't exist and, therefore, couldn't happen.

Society as arsonist? Had the local villagers set fire to the story in a frenzy to erase any trace of its existence? No, they didn't have that much power because here I was…inside the story.

Think. What happens if you can't burn something to get rid of it? You bury it.

I needed a map and a shovel. "X" marks the spot. I was on a quest for story treasure. What a crock of shit.

Life was not what I was prepared for, nor was it what I had been told to expect. It was difficult not to feel betrayed, angry and lied to.

* * *

Our last day of retreat was when Johnny Netti's girlfriend discovered our sanctuary. She was, needless to say, not pleased to find him chilling with two girls, scantily dressed and wet from a recent swim. Frances and I tried to explain we were just friends with Johnny, but his girlfriend turned on her heel and marched away.

At first Johnny did nothing. Just let her go off. He said that she needed to get over herself. But the more time that went by, the more nervous he got. Finally, to save face, he said he'd been spending too much time away from his band. We told him goodbye.

That afternoon, Frances and I finished the rest of the beer and with a lazy buzz, we fell asleep in the long grass, my head resting on her shoulder.

* * *

Frances and I decided it was better if we went back to our classes. We were both eighteen and could write our own notes for our absences, but we had missed a lot of school and I was in danger of not doing well if I didn't do some quick catch-up.

I didn't see Frances much at school, our schedules were different for one thing, but mostly I think it was because our relationship wasn't of school. It was designed for freedom and dreams. And freedom and dreams don't have much to do with high school.

Johnny Netti, I discovered, had been living with his girlfriend for the past year. He played music and she paid the bills. She must have laid down the law because when I passed him in the halls I received only a nod. But it didn't bother me. I understood his position, and frankly, I kind of pitied him.

My first full day back, Patty stopped dead in her tracks, plopped her hands on her hips, and spoke so loudly that it reverberated down the halls and people stopped and stared. "Well, well, well…if she doesn't grace us with her presence!"

I reddened and gave her a look, but I was glad to be missed. She linked her arm in mine and started talking nonstop about her life. I listened only partly to her words and instead relaxed into the rhythm of her chatter. I smiled and made plans to get a hamburger with her at lunch before heading to class.

* * *

I waited ten minutes for Patty before allowing myself to get really concerned that she wasn't going to show up. When she finally came running up to me, all distressed, my first thought was, why did Patty always seem so distressed? Concern beyond that never even entered my mind. Funny how some exceptionally serious moments are never foreseen.

"Why are you just standing there!"

"Why the hell do you think? I'm waiting for you."

"Oh, Ella!" She said this as though I were an imbecile. She pulled me away from the wall I was leaning against. "Look." She pointed up at the clock tower, which was what I was leaning against.

I looked up and had no small anxiety attack when I saw Renee sitting up there. One foot slung over the edge, swaying back and forth.

"Go do something!" Patty screamed at me.

But I was already on my way up. People were starting to gather around. They were expecting another suicide dive. We already had one at the beginning of that year, this small skinny guy who was only fourteen. I didn't know him personally, but I remembered seeing him lying there, his head in a pool of blood. I couldn't take my eyes off his scattered school textbooks, and I just kept thinking, why did he jump with his books? Who commits suicide carrying history and science books?

When I got to the top, I saw that Renee was now standing up, hanging on to the molding to keep her balance. She saw me as I stepped onto the roof and started walking toward her.

"Did you say mother may I?"

I stopped because I didn't know if she was serious. I decided she wasn't and I tried a smile. "Renee—"

"Did you?" she shouted at me.

I lowered my head in humiliation. "Mother may I come closer to you?"

"No," she said flatly, "you may never, as long as you live, come closer to me."

I was hurt, irritated, and tired of the game. "Just stop it!" I took a step forward.

"Ever! Not ever! Don't take one step closer. Do you hear me? I hate you!"

That stopped me all right, like a fist in my chest.

Her body began to shake. For the first time, I really looked at Renee, and that's when I noticed she was drunk—the price I paid for still feeling too guilty to look at her. There was a bottle of Jack Daniel's at her feet. "You never get drunk. What's wrong with you?" And it was true. No matter how much everyone around her was drinking, she barely ever drank. I could count the amount of times on one hand that I saw her drunk.

"Oh," Renee laughed and swayed. "I'm drunk. I wondered what was wrong with me." She had a dizzy spell and tried to sit down on the ledge, but her balance was bad and she started to fall off the side.

My heart lurched. I barely made it in time, grabbing Renee by the arm and setting her upright. At first she was too dizzy to notice me next to her, but in the next moment she pulled her arm from me and pushed me away. She looked angry but also ready to cry, and I had never, in all the time I'd known Renee, seen her cry. I couldn't help but watch her with intense curiosity.

She covered her face with her arm. I think to wipe away the tears that started. "You left me alone," she said in a small voice.

I was struck dumb by the size of that truth. At the same time, I was shocked that I had that much of an impact. Renee was always so self-sufficient. How could I matter this much? For a hair of a second I considered telling her everything that happened, but my mind felt inaccessible and I couldn't quite remember everything—like how childhood memories will evade you. Then I remembered that I was dealing with a depressed, drunk person sitting on the edge of a roof. I searched for something that wouldn't be a lie. I just couldn't tell a lie.

"I've had things on my mind and I needed some time alone," I said.

Renee's expression changed like a kaleidoscope and she was immediately, and sincerely, concerned. "What is it? Are you all right?"

Guilt ran through my veins like I was hooked up to an IV of the stuff. "I'm fine," I said, looking over the edge and wondering why I didn't have the nerve to throw myself off. I hated myself and changed the subject. "Tell me what's wrong."

Renee, even drunk, was sharp. She knew I was hiding something. She looked away from me and put her defenses back up.

I didn't want to lose connection with her so I gave her something to chew on. "I've been worried about what I'm going to do after high school."

That must have struck a nerve because I saw tears again in her eyes. "I didn't get in."

I knew right away that she meant the art school she applied to. "Oh shit. That sucks. I'm so sorry."

"I have the grades and the talent...but I lack the *character* of their students." She laughed but not a real laugh. "Isn't it funny that of all things I would be accused of a lack of character?"

"Why would they think that?"

"I lack character because..." She trailed off and sat staring. Just when I thought she wasn't going to finish she said, "Because I do things that, at the time, seem important."

I felt like I'd been hit over the head with a two-by-four. "Your suspensions?" Of course, that would make sense. Why had it never occurred to me before?

She didn't answer me because she was in her own world. Again she said, "It seemed important at the time."

Jesus Christ, it was pathetic! Renee unsure and questioning her actions? I could take anything from her but *that*—I needed *that* to be consistent. She was the Rebel Queen.

"It was important! Nothing you did was wrong, Renee." I was close to shaking her until her teeth rattled, so I sat on my hands. "Besides, there are other art schools, you know. Ones that don't have such a big stick up their ass."

She gave me a tired, fuck-off look.

I breathed a heavy sigh and set my mind to being a friend, not someone who gave lame advice.

She crossed her arms and weaved back and forth. "Why are you here?"

"Gee, I don't know, maybe it was the sight of your legs dangling off the clock tower."

"Oh, that...Well, you didn't think I was going to jump, did you?"

"Renee, I'm worried about you."

"Isn't that sweet. Well, now you see that I'm fine, nothing to have worried your pretty little head over. You can leave now."

She damn well meant to be demeaning and it pissed me off, but I ignored it and concentrated on getting her off the roof.

"Let's get you down from here, huh?" I tried to take her by the hand.

She pulled away. "Don't you dare patronize me!"

"I didn't think I was." I was stunned by her hostility.

"Well you did."

"I'm sorry."

"I don't need anyone's help and, contrary to what you think, I especially don't need yours."

That hurt. But if I had a few cuts and scrapes, she was bleeding internally. "I know you don't need my help, but I want to give it."

"What makes you think I would take it?"

I inched closer to her. "I just think you will, that's all." I put my arm around her shoulder and held my breath, waiting for her to push me off the side where I would fall to my well-deserved death. But she didn't. Instead, she sat there uncertainly, kind of disoriented and confused. Finally, she turned and buried her face in my neck. She sobbed so silently, her body heaving just so slightly, that you would think she was paralyzed and this was all her agonized body could produce.

I put my other arm around her and she let me coax her off the edge and onto the safe, flat part, of the roof. I rocked her back and forth, running my hand up and down her back and through her hair. I told her it would be all right.

I kept holding her even when Principal Monroe appeared. I couldn't let her go because I felt I had to protect her. She felt so delicate and shattered after having fallen all that way from her pedestal.

CHAPTER ELEVEN

Rock It like Gidget

Patty's bedroom has a canopy bed. That pretty much says it all. I guess the abundance of movie star and rock posters is also worth mentioning. The point is that being in Patty's room is like being in a rerun of a damn *Gidget* episode.

I was lying on Patty's bed. She was sitting at her vanity table with her feet propped up, cotton balls between each toe. She was painting her toenails—I swear to God—bubble gum pink.

"Patty, you cannot possibly paint your toes that color."

"Why not?"

"Because someone might see them."

"Don't you like this color?"

I rolled on my back and groaned. I stared at the canopy. I was spending more time with Patty since *That Night*, and especially since the incident with Renee on the clock tower. It wasn't that odd, especially now that Renee was being forced into counseling since she "tried to take her life." Now, whenever I saw her at school, she was odd. Renee, who had always held her head high, walked with her head down. She would hardly ever talk, and when she did it was only to Patty or me. It depressed me to no end.

"Do you really hate this color?"

"Pretty much."

"Are you going tell me what's wrong with you?"

I wasn't surprised. I knew that she knew something was wrong.

"All my friends are falling apart," she said.

"No we're not."

She gave me a look. "Yes, they are."

"Yes, we are," I admitted.

I considered telling her about *That Night* because I knew she wouldn't hold anything against me. It was Patty's strongest virtue. She gave everyone a fair shot and allowed for a person's blunders. It was like she gave out a certain number of tokens that were meant to be played and lost, giving the gambler a leeway that meant they didn't have to lose everything on just one go-around. Still, I didn't want to tell Patty about *That Night*, not yet. But it was good to know that, at least with Patty, some of my mistakes might be "on the house."

I definitely knew I wasn't ready to talk about the Diane part of *That Night*, or my more general concern about girls. But if the time came, Patty would be the first person I'd tell. I guess this says something about her I hadn't really realized.

Patty's window was open to allow in the cool breeze, and on one of those breezes, soft music floated up. It was faint at first, but it became progressively louder.

"What is that?" Patty asked.

I jumped up and went to the window. Two stories below Patty's window stood Gerrard in some ridiculous costume carrying a ghetto blaster. On closer inspection, he was in some sort of costume and looked like a throwback to some poor suitor of yesteryear. "Oh, my God." Gerrard had fully entered through the gates of Nerddom.

"What is it?" Patty asked again.

The music to Blue Oyster Cult's "Don't Fear the Reaper" began and Gerrard sang along with the song, gesturing up to the window in flamboyant arcs. He kept knocking the big fancy hat off his head.

I was a good ten paces beyond amusement and inching toward horrified.

"Well, what is it?" Patty was dying of curiosity.

"I'm not sure I can adequately describe this scene." I waved her over.

Patty waddled over on her heels so her toes wouldn't get messed up. She looked down at her suitor. "Gerrard!" she said to me. "Is that Gerrard?"

I nodded. I didn't open my mouth for fear I'd let loose a laugh that would shoot me around the room like a balloon.

"Gerrard?" She squinted down at the ground like Mrs. MaGoo. "Gerrard, what is it with you?"

The full moon shone down upon the lovesick Gerrard. He let the words of the song go by without him and replied to his true love, a hand over his heart, "It is I, my love!"

I moaned and silent laughter wracked my insides.

Patty put her hands on her hips like a mother wanting an answer. "Gerrard, what the hell are you doing down there?"

"It is my love that has brought me here. It bursts inside my heart so that I can no longer hide it from you." He threw his hands skyward and knocked off his hat yet again.

"Gerrard, are you doing one of those Cyrano de Bergerac things? Is someone down there in the bushes with you?" Patty leaned farther out the window trying to find Gerrard's accomplice.

"It is only I and my love that brings me here, begging for what small crumbs you might throw my way." Gerrard gestured up to the open window.

"I think that costume belongs to the theater department." I was suddenly aware of this not-so-important fact. "I think Brent Scoper wore it in last year's production of *Romeo and Juliet*."

Patty gave me a perplexed double take.

"I know, it looks like the *Three Musketeers*, but the theater department doesn't have a lot of money." I shrugged.

She shushed me. "Can this be the same Gerrard?"

"It is one and the same, my love!" Gerrard sang out.

"Why are you such a nerd at school, and so poetic—" Patty leaned dreamily out the window, "—and smooth now?"

"You've whacked out," I told Patty. "You've gone right over the ribbon and bow edge."

Patty punched me with her middle knuckle pushed out, giving me a gnarly charlie horse that hurt like hell!

Gerrard put his hat over his heart. "My affection had made me mute, but now it grants me a tongue! How can I control the will of such a great love?"

"Gerrard!" Patty said delightedly.

"Please, say you will spend an evening with me and take away my misery!" Gerrard pleaded.

"Well, I don't know." Patty was, per the rules, now playing hard to get.

"I throw myself upon your mercy," Gerrard said, stretching his neck out further on the butcher block. "I would gladly kill myself after an evening with you, as such happiness could never come again."

"Oh, brother. That is just it." I rolled my eyes and received another pop in the arm. I could feel the knotted bruise swelling.

"Don't do that! Yes! Yes, I'll go out with you!" Patty cried down like the Virgin Queen, even as she was beating me to a pulp.

Gerrard was giddy. "I'll pick you up tomorrow at seven o'clock. Until then, my love, I will serenade you!" He continued lip-syncing to Blue Oyster Cult.

"Oh! Can you believe it? I'm being serenaded! God, this is so exciting!" Patty, between fluttering her hand over her chest as though she would faint, managed to waddle back to the vanity table and punch me in the arm.

"Would you stop that!"

"Where do you think he'll take me?"

I checked my eyelids to make sure they were open, snapping my fingers in front of my face. Nothing happened. I had to accept that I was awake.

"I never realized how cute he was until I saw him with that hat on. Isn't he cute in that hat? Didn't you think so?"

"Patty," I said, finding my voice, "your life is like some kind of warped *Gidget* rerun."

Patty fluttered her hand over her chest again and said with real glee, "I know!"

CHAPTER TWELVE

REO Speedwagon Stepford Wife

It took me about three weeks to catch up with all the work I'd missed during my extended field trip with Frances Riley and Johnny Netti. During that time I didn't see much of anyone, or anything, except the inside of my room. My dad never knew I cut classes, nor would he have cared.

One night there was a rap at my window.

"We're going to a warehouse party, wanna come?" Patty asked.

Warehouse parties were fun. It meant there would be a live band and tons of people.

"Come on," she implored, "you've been locked up here for ages!"

"I need to change clothes."

Patty nodded. She understood the importance of proper attire.

* * *

The warehouse was way out in the middle of nowhere. The music was loud and people were outside as well as inside, smoking pot and drinking beer they brought themselves. It was too much to expect beer to be provided at a gathering that large. It was enough that the party-giver managed to get a band, which was playing a mixture of popular rock songs and their own music. They weren't too bad. It occurred to me that out of all the warehouse parties I'd been to, I'd never known who threw them.

Patty and Gerrard were staring goo-goo-eyed at each other as we entered the large structure. It was dimly lighted, as befitting these gatherings, and I looked around to see what was what.

The band was at the far end on a makeshift stage. There was a group of people listening to them, but not like you'd see at a concert where people flipped out and lost their minds, they were so in love with the band. To the right of the door was a bunch of people I recognized, people I went to school with, and they were talking in groups, laughing and flirting with each other. They were dressed "properly" and they were "properly" attractive.

To my left were the outsiders. Some were Punk. Some were Rockers. Some were the stoners and waste-cases (the ones who went to my school but who skipped classes and hung out in garages). Their lives were cars, music, motorcycles and drugs. They all looked kind of different and crazy, but were just as beautiful as the "properly" attired insider group.

Gerrard and Patty went to the right and talked to some friends. I walked in farther, to the back of the group watching the band. I kept kind of glancing around to see if I knew anyone. That's when the hair caught my eye. Long loose curls, wild, and when Diane Lacey turned around, I saw the self-confidence there in her body. Her head thrown back as she laughed, her hand keeping the beat of the music on her thigh, she smiled broadly and without her usual self-consciousness. Her clothes were different too—more casual and less put together, and it made her more attractive, if that were humanly possible. She still looked wholesome, like she could do a "milk does a body good" commercial, but she had lost her girl-next-door innocence. I was just considering the pros and cons of going over and talking to her, when I saw her lean closer to the girl standing next to her. She whispered in her ear in a way that suggested she enjoyed lingering there. The girl laughed and touched Diane's hand and in one boiling-hot moment, split-hair-of-a-second-explosion, I wanted to go rip the girl's hair from her head. I kid you not, I wanted to scratch her eyes out and throw her far away from Diane. It was, without a doubt, the girliest moment of my life. I must have been outright staring because the girl was startled enough to point me out to Diane when our eyes met. Diane turned and looked, and when her eyes met mine, she was surprised—in that way I've seen her so often be surprised by me—but then she actually smirked.

"Do you want a beer?"

An arm came around me and Frances smiled down at me with her soft blue eyes.

"Hey you!" And I gave her a genuine hug of hello. But I couldn't stop myself from looking over my shoulder at Diane. Her expression was different now—disgruntled, her arms crossed. It was my turn to smirk.

I turned back to Frances and smiled. The band's set ended. She pushed the brim of her cowboy hat back so she could bring her face closer to mine.

"So, how about you and I go somewhere else." She smiled big so that there would be no mistaking her meaning.

I was shocked, but refreshed by the sheer honesty of her approach, and I laughed nervously. She put both arms around me and continued her sultry smile. The suggestion in her body language elicited a pleasurable twinge from me in a place I didn't know was an involuntary muscle. My breath caught in my throat. This needed to be explored. I was—and wasn't—surprised to hear myself agree to leave with her.

Then I felt a sensation I can't really explain. It was like a chill going up my spine. I turned around a saw him. That guy, the one who told me he was my Fairy Godfather. He was standing near the entrance to the warehouse. He waved his wand at the stage and raised his eyebrows, like he was trying to tell me something. I said to Frances, "Do you see that guy standing over there? He looks punk. He has a wand and he's looking at us."

Frances eyed me. "A wand?" She looked. "The only person I see is that stoner guy with the big 'fro."

I saw the guy she meant, but that other guy, okay my Fairy Godfather—Christ, I felt stupid even thinking it in my own head—was standing right next to him. "No, that other guy, standing right next to him."

Frances looked again. "I don't see anyone else."

I turned and looked and he was gone. "He was there a second ago."

"Is he important to you?"

"No," I said. "I don't know. Maybe."

Frances moved her hands from my waist and said, "Do you want to go find him?" I realized then that she thought I was into him.

"No, no, not like that. It's a friend, that's all." I reached out and brought her hand back to me.

We turned around, ready to leave, Frances's hand on the small of my back, her fingers roaming, making small circles, making it hard for me to walk and think at the same time, when I recognized Altman's voice.

Over the loudspeaker his voice boomed. "Everyone? Hello? Is thing on? I have an announcement to make."

I swiveled around. "Wait a minute." He was up on the stage talking into the microphone.

"I'm not very good at this sort of thing, so I'll just say it. Um, I asked Renee Hammond to marry me."

There was whooping and catcalling from the crowd. I felt punched and winded. It was the first time in my life I ever felt like I could actually collapse. My knees went weak and Frances caught me by the waist and held me up.

"And she just said yes." He was smiling like a little boy who just got the toy he wanted for Christmas.

People near the stage clapped and yelled out their approval.

"Come on up, honey." He gestured and Renee was pushed up onto the stage by enthusiastic hands. She was wearing some kind of flower dress.

Really? A flower dress? Are you fucking kidding me?

Patty came up from behind me and looked at me with concern. "God, Ella. Look at her. She looks like a Stepford Wife."

I wanted to cry. She looked like a fucking joke! She was wearing some godawful flowery dress like she was straight out of a rerun of *Little House on the Prairie*. I shook, feeling sick to my stomach. "She can't marry that bastard," I told Patty. I forgot Patty didn't know he was a cheating son of a bitch, but it didn't matter because she nodded as though she agreed.

On stage Renee kissed Altman's offered lips, then bowed her head so she wouldn't have to look at the crowd that was applauding her so sweetly. To many people they were the ideal couple, but couldn't anyone see how weird Renee was being?

"Maybe you should go talk to her," Patty said.

"Maybe." Then I remembered Frances, and was embarrassed now that Patty was standing so close.

But Frances seemed to understand because she took my hand and covered it with her other hand. "It's okay. Call if you need me?" She kissed me on the cheek and whispered in my ear, "Don't think I'm not disappointed." She made her way, weaving through the crowd with one look back and a smile for me.

I gave Patty the eye to see if she noticed anything, but she was looking through the crowd for Renee.

"You know, he's a cheater. Gerrard told me he goes out on her all the time," Patty said.

"I know," I said under my breath. I looked over for Diane, but she was gone.

When I got to where Renee and Altman were, they were surrounded by a group of people. When I finally made my way to Renee's side, she looked at me with big sad eyes. I don't think she knew she looked this way.

"I wanna talk to you," I whispered.

"Go ahead."

Altman stopped his conversation with another guy and looked at me. He was scared. Boy, was he scared.

"Alone," I whispered.

"Ella, I just got engaged. Didn't you hear? Now isn't the best time. Besides, you haven't even congratulated me. You are going to congratulate me, aren't you?"

"Not before I talk to you."

She let go of Altman's arm and turned toward me. When she did this she held on to me, as if for balance, and whispered into my ear, "I'm pregnant." She looked at me with wounded eyes. "And," she smiled pathetically, "I expect you to be my maid of honor. Now are you going to congratulate me?"

"Congratulations."

She put a hand on my cheek. "Cheer up, you're going to be an auntie."

I took her hand from my cheek, not meanly, but I couldn't bear it there. "No," I said, and I was so horribly sad. "You need to come to your senses." And I walked away from her before I had to take one more second of those sad eyes and that flowered dress.

The lead singer announced they were going to play a song for the newly engaged couple. Honestly, they started playing an awful version of REO Speedwagon's "Roll with the Changes." Not only was it an awful rendition, but completely opposite of who Renee was. It was like Altman was swallowing her whole. She was to become his REO Speedwagon Stepford wife.

On my way out, I saw my Fairy Godfather again, leaning against the entrance of the warehouse, in the same place he so conveniently disappeared from moments ago. Where was he when I really needed him? He was nothing like the Fairy Godmothers in the fairy tales. He didn't give me help when I needed it, he didn't swoop down and rescue me when I was in trouble. He just let me drown in this awful story. It was like there was a silent ticking bomb in my heart and seeing him detonated it. I walked up to him and pushed him. "Why did you act like you cared about me when all along you were helping her?"

He caught himself from falling backward and stood up taller. "I have the ability to help more than one person."

I was on the verge of anger mixed with tears. "But when you went to her, that's when you stopped helping me."

"No," he said softly, "I never stopped. You disappeared. And in your absence the stories don't stop, they move on without you. You've lost your way. I can only help you when you're in the story and now you've left the story all together. It's up to you to find your way back. When you do, I'll be here."

"Then help me find my way back." I knew there were tears running down my cheeks.

"I wish I could, my little unicorn. That's not my role. But you have someone who will help you, just pay attention."

I felt completely alone. I made my way out of the warehouse, swearing to myself that I wouldn't even try to figure out what he meant, that I'd rather live the rest of my life in a cave than give him the satisfaction of admitting he was right and that I was completely lost.

CHAPTER THIRTEEN

Joni Mitchell Under the Oak Tree

There was a month until graduation that I began to think of as *The Interim*. During that time, I decided I would try to figure out what to do with my life. Concentrate on my future.

But all I kept thinking about was my past.

And so, regardless of all my concern over my foggy future, I was haunted by memories. I remembered things I didn't even know that I knew, like the time way back when I was in ninth grade when I hung out with Cherish. She came over late at night and we'd watch *The Twilight Zone* and *The Outer Limits*. We liked to lie on our stomachs, only a foot away from the television, until she invariably got scared by some horrible "monster" and ended up lying on my back, her body running the length of mine. It was reassuring to have her weight on me, and we laughed about it and all, but there was *something else* too. Something I felt when the laughter stopped and she was still on my back, staying there until the station break. And the *something else* part of my memories was like the swallows coming back to Capistrano.

It was a darkening of the sky as recollections flew back to roost. I went through photographs, letters and yearbooks, anything that might flush out a memory. Most shocking? The flock of memories that surrounded Renee.

Renee at a party, she stands in a hallway and reaches out for me to hold her.

We cuddle in the backseat of a car, on the way to someplace or another.

Renee holds me while I bury my nose in her neck because I am drunk.

Staying the night at Renee's house after parties and falling asleep next to her and holding her hand.

Lots of things, tons of them just like these. Drunken moments. It was typical girl stuff and really no big deal. But it was the *something else* part of the memories that haunted me: the smell of her hair, the softness of her neck, the touch of her fingers on my skin. It left me with a longing and some deep melancholy. I knew then that alcohol was often necessary in order to steal her touch.

But I didn't know how it was for her. Did she feel these things? And she rarely drank.

I recalled the prom and our wrestling in the field, and the knot that formed in my stomach. At the time, I thought for certain that she felt something too. And we weren't drunk, so it was different. Still, with Renee, I couldn't prove anything to myself, so I really knew nothing.

It was with Diane and Frances that I gained my proof, and regained my sanity. It was they who reassured me I had not lost my mind. Crazy, that's all I kept thinking. How do you know you're just not crazy?

My despair over Renee's engagement to Altman was confusing. I didn't know if I was upset over Altman's infidelity, and his general unworthiness of her or...had I, somewhere along the way, fallen in love with her?

The largeness of this prospect shut me down, like a surge of electricity that has tripped the main switch. I was powered down and running on auxiliary. I woke up at night from dreams

I couldn't remember, sat straight up, my body wracked with sweat and exhaustion, as though I'd just run a marathon. My inner workings were in such turmoil that I could no longer even count on my sleep to replenish me. The cycle of thinking became a vicious loop I could not escape from, with one thought leading to another. Always starting with an innocent recollection, it would turn into that one concrete action—the kiss with Diane—leading to a replay of *That Night*, until the guilt and confusion become unbearable.

But as the weeks went by, I slept more and more because my wakeful musings were more disturbing than my sleeping ones. And so I shut my curtains in the middle of the day and tried to escape my mind. My dad would knock on the door when he came in for lunch in the afternoon. I told him I was feeling sick but not to worry, I just needed to sleep. When he asked if I needed to go to the doctor, I wanted to laugh. Was there a cure for this? And if there were would I want it?

What did my supposed Fairy Godfather say?

"...pretty soon you won't recognize yourself. You'll feel like a mythical being, the types you've heard about in fairy tales: unicorns, elves, sprites. You'll begin to question who you are because you've never seen another of your kind in this human world, so you won't believe you're real."

He meant gay? Was I now a mythical creature that lived in the shadowy peripheries of the dark forest where other villagers were afraid to tread? There were stories, folk tales and urban legends. They were whispered in hushed tones, talked about in private quarters between trusted parties. I knew it wasn't fit social conversation.

"But you are real, my little unicorn..."

A little too precious, but I got the point. So was I the only unicorn? Were there others?

He was right. Gay had been forced to the shadowy outer edges of the world. Why no longer mattered. I doubted anyone remembered, nor was that story likely to be written down. But I knew it was dangerous to be gay in this world, knew it instinctively. To show yourself was to risk fear and all that came from that fear, maybe even violence and death. At the very least, you would be banished back to the dark forest, told to stay with your own kind and to never come back into the world of these humans or risk losing it all. This I knew without being told. I was in danger. So, my Fairy Godfather, I say to you, I know to stay cloaked and not show my true unicorn self.

But what about my story? *My* story.

How do I begin to tell a story I've never heard before? There was no template. No story structure. How should I know what happens to the characters? Do they live happily ever after? Are they banished? If so, where do they go?

And this brought me to the most terrible thought of all.

How can I prove I exist without a story?

Who would know I passed this way? Yes, I was a thief. But how the hell do I steal a story I can't find? A story as mysterious as buried treasure?

There were too many questions with no answers.

I had no choice. Clearly, the story would need to be made up as I went along.

But I was scared, so it had to be a whispered story, told in darkened rooms—but among whom? Who would hear this story?

And then I was angry. Why shouldn't it be a proud story? Told in the light of day, among the respectable townsfolk in the fairy tale marketplace and square, where the people gathered to tell of great heroes and their deeds. Not a story, if told in public, under the scrutiny of ignorant villagers, that had women covering children's ears and ushering them back to the safety of home and hearth where the acceptable stories resided out in the open, on family bookshelves (regardless how many contained children being eaten, monsters that lived under the bed or violent atrocities).

But I knew. It was in stone. This story never wavered in the retelling: the princess only ever falls in love with the prince.

It concerned me much less that my story was "shameful or bad" than did the seriousness implied by the story's *sheer absence*.

Not having a story was a fate comparable to death.

Death implied nonexistence and stories implied existence.

If a story was told and the creature vilified, there was the possibility of redemption or rebellion. But when a person, someone, *me*, had no story at all, that meant you were not even worth acknowledging. You were of such little consequence that a story about how awful you were didn't even exist, so the creature (no matter how beautiful) was worse than nothing. What is worse than nothing? Not even death is worse than nothing. At least in death you can still have a story, told and retold.

Which means, I concluded, if you had this unspoken story, you were worse off than dead, because you didn't exist even while you were alive. You were not even worthy of the most minor narrative. I would have rather been a villain! I could reclaim, resurrect and retell their story. Better than not existing at all.

So, yes, it was the great silent void that scared me.

As little Cinderella, I rebelled but lost my mother. Still, it was a great story of rebellion. I resurrected myself as Knight to the Rebel Queen and redeemed and reclaimed what I thought was my true self, my true story. And it was a worthy story, told loudly, proudly throughout the kingdom's courtyards. I was respected and revered. Who was I now? Left all alone at the edge of the dark forest, revealed as a mythical creature (not even *I* knew I was), and I carried in my hands a story—muted, foreign and untellable to a soul, much less a kingdom.

So, again, if there were there a cure for this would I want it?

Unquestionably and empathically...no.

Why? Because of the brilliant, shiny realization I couldn't stop looking at: As miserable and heartbroken as I was, for the first time in my life I experienced a glimmer of what it was like to be me. I was awake. Present. I no longer sensed I was playacting a part on stage where I could never remember the script and some tech person was always feeding me the lines.

I was alive. Finally.

* * *

The only people I saw during *The Interim* were Patty and Gerrard, whom I took an occasional meal with, and Frances. Even my time with Ricky disintegrated.

One day Frances jumped the cinder block wall in my backyard and asked me to come outside and sit with her. I asked how she knew where I lived, but she liked to tease me and wouldn't tell, and after all it couldn't have been information that hard to come by.

She changed the Ramones album I was listening to and put on Joni Mitchell. She said I needed a break from my rebellion. I looked at the album cover. Frances kind of looked like a tall Joni Mitchell.

We watched the sunset that night and she told me she was leaving after graduation to do Peace Corps work in Central America. Unlike many volunteers, she wanted her life experience before college. She said it would "settle" her. And she certainly had enough agricultural background to be accepted as a volunteer. Hell, she was probably a find.

I was sad to think of her leaving and told her so. She patted my hand and said I was leaving too, so we would both miss each other. When I told her I didn't know what I wanted to do, she laughed. I mean she laughed like she thought I was precious and should be cherished. I didn't understand, but I certainly didn't mind being regarded in that way, so I let her cherish me.

After that, she came to my backyard every night at sunset and we sat on the wall to watch the sun go down. Often we didn't say much. She started bringing a bag of sunflower seeds and I would bring out a pitcher of iced tea. Whenever she left, usually not long after the sun had set, I wondered if she would ever bring up the night of the warehouse. Every night I waited, thinking maybe she would just lean over and kiss me the way Diane had.

I nearly gave up hope, and decided I had misinterpreted her meaning the night of the warehouse, when one night, just as the sun set, I put my arm around her. I was feeling sad and wanted to touch her, needed to be comforted. The moment I did this, she turned to me and asked if she could kiss me. I didn't want to be asked, I just wanted her to do it—though perhaps that is exactly why she asked, so I could no longer hide from my persistent craving. I said yes. She hopped down from the wall and helped me down too, not because I couldn't on my own, but because she had turned chivalrous, taking the role of my champion. She guided me to the large oak tree and pulled me down to the ground, and there, she kissed me.

* * *

Later, as she slipped my shorts over my hips, I noticed her looking down at them as though they were precious and fragile, and I realized that I didn't see myself that way. But it seemed like all the girls who had tried, and sometimes failed, to love me, were all larger-than-life. I was always tilting my head back to look up into their eyes. And though I've never considered myself some overly delicate creature, how could I not when all these larger-than-life girls surrounded me? And how will I survive them, I thought, before I was taken out of my mind and into my body again, with Frances pulling me along as easily as a puppet on a string. She mastered my body that easily.

* * *

Every night Frances came to my house at sunset, and every night I lay down with her under the oak tree just as soon as the sun set under the vast summer sky. It was tender, but urgent too, and though I cared about Ricky, it was a very different kind of lovemaking that went on under the oak tree, and I knew, in some way, that it was the truth underscoring all my desire. I searched, but I found no bottom to that untapped well.

We didn't talk much, so busy with other things, but I did ask her not to go away to Central America. She just smiled at me, kindly, lovingly, refusing to give rational reasons why she must go or couldn't stay. And that's when I knew I loved her. I told her I did. "I love you," I said. And she moved further into the middle ground of my heart.

When I imagined this gentle giant in a foreign land, her courage seared my soul. I kept wishing I had her certainty, her focus, because my life seemed like a dismal proposition. I tried to see my life in different scenarios, but instead found my mind wandering, like the stones we once skimmed across the glassy surface of the lake.

I listened to that Joni Mitchell album every day for a month.

CHAPTER FOURTEEN

Miss Perfect is a Lesbo

There was only a week until graduation and I was on my way to my last class, when this girl, her face I knew, but not her name, stopped me in the hall to give me the buzz on Diane. She said that Diane Lacey was having it out with Chad Walker, that he was mad and pushing her around. Blood rose to my face like a geyser. I was crazy-mad, and asked her where. She assured me it was all over with and that Diane was fine. I relaxed enough to ask what happened.

She sidled up next to me, all excited. "He found out she was a lesbian!"

I nearly fell over. Considering the sheer overkill of my thoughts on the matter, I was surprised that I never prepared myself for such a moment.

The girl, judging from my slack jaw, was convinced that I was scandalized too. "I know!" she said, "is that unbelievable, or what? Miss Goody Two-shoes, Miss Perfect is a lesbo!"

"But how does he know?"

The girl gave me the you're-not-going-to-believe-this look. "I don't know how, but here's the best part: Along comes this new guy—dresses weird, I don't know his name—and he decks Chad flat! I heard he couldn't get up for ten minutes and they almost had to call an ambulance!"

Now I was becoming scandalized. "Oh, my God." Was it, could it be him? My Fairy Godfather? Was he real? People could see him? Be punched by him? Maybe I wasn't crazy, or maybe she meant someone else.

"And there's one other thing." She said this in a way that suggested I might not want to hear it. "I heard that your name came up a few times."

"My name?" I felt like there was a little man tap dancing on my heart.

"I guess Chad seems to think Diane has a…I don't know quite how to say this…a kind of, like, thing for you." She said it as though it was ridiculous, but she watched me like a hawk.

"Well," I said and shrugged to indicate it was indeed ridiculous, "I am cute."

She laughed as though that was just the funniest thing and swiped at my arm playfully. "Oh, Ella."

I felt sick to my stomach.

* * *

I went to my class and couldn't concentrate at all. There was this terrible screaming voice in my head. At first I only felt its cadence, but then the words became clear: *They can't be together!* I thought I was losing my mind. I cradled my head and rubbed my temples to quiet the scream.

Realities.

Just like that, I understood. I had created two realities, two stories, because one had not been safe with the other. But something went wrong, some unknown phenomenon must have occurred, creating this natural social disaster of epic proportions—my stories were going to collide.

* * *

I was just about to walk into the girls' bathroom when Renee appeared out of nowhere.

"I want to talk to you." She was angry.

"Okay," I said as she pulled me all the way into the bathroom.

"I want to know if something happened between you and Altman during our last trip to the beach house." Point-blank, no hemming or hawing.

I felt utter despair before roaring anger replaced it. I threw a heavy textbook at the mirror and broke it. Did I really wish it could have been forgotten and never spoken of? Yes, with all my heart. Where was the justice in the world, that something so pathetic and unworthy could have the ability to ruin lives?

I always imagined this conversation would happen in the middle of an intimate talk. We are feeling really close to each other and I confess the weighty stone I carry in my heart. We both cry and I tell her how confused I had been and that, in fact, it was detestable to me, and certainly nothing could be closer to the truth. I don't even like Altman. She puts her arms around me and tells me it's okay, that it was all a series of unfortunate events.

Well, I certainly have a rich fantasy life because nothing in my current reality came remotely close to my imaginings.

I can't express how close I came to lying, to weighing the loss of Renee against the sin of a lie, and coming out with the lie. With great trepidation, I confessed. "Yes, something happened."

She turned her face to the tiled wall.

I tried to explain how bizarre the situation had been but I couldn't really explain it without telling her about Diane or my general confusion about girls, and I wasn't ready for that conversation. So, in the end, all that could possibly matter to her was that I confirmed it.

She turned back to me with tears in her eyes and raged, "How could you do this to me? You're my best friend! How could you lie? How could you betray me?"

I understood her anger since it had once been mine. There was a time when I was at that very point myself, and I asked myself the same questions. But I wasn't there anymore. Now I was trying to accept that it happened. Accept that there was nothing I could do to fix it. But it was so hard. I always believed, no matter how bad things got, if I just tried—*did something*—I could always make things okay. I was her Knight and there was never anything I wouldn't do to protect her. So, how could I accept my lack of ability now to do anything?

"When were you going to tell me? Ever? Were you ever going to tell me?" She pushed me against the wall.

"I'm sorry. It's not what you think. I've been really confused. I was really drunk and I just…I can't really explain it to you. It's this complicated thing…" I was trying really hard to explain without saying what was happening to me lately with girls, but I couldn't figure out how to say it.

"How is there an excuse for that? There's no excuse!"

That's when I got angry, when I started to rationalize. "I told you it was a mistake—I fucked up! Is that all I am to you now? That one mistake? Forget who I've been, forget what our friendship's been? All it comes down to is that one fucking, humiliating, miserable mistake?"

She stopped yelling at me and I took the opportunity to leave before it started back up. She didn't try to stop me as I walked out the bathroom door.

When I came out, I saw Altman sitting on a bench just outside of the bathroom. His head was down, and when he looked up at me, there was something in his body language that I had never seen in him before, some kind of submission. And that's when I saw him for who he truly was. I couldn't believe I'd never noticed it before. He was completely afraid. He wasn't a jerk because he was an egotistical son of a bitch. He was a jerk because he had no self-confidence and he was afraid. I was stunned and, for the first time, I felt compassion toward him. Yeah, he did awful things all the time, but he was really damaged and scared. It was sort of sad.

Then I saw Chad standing nearby. He was so fucking smug—and so thoroughly enjoying life at that moment—that I knew he was the one who told Renee. No doubt he heard enough bragging from Altman (though mostly lies I'm sure) and when he couldn't have Diane, he decided he would destroy me, believing I was responsible for his misery. The fool. I hated him. And suddenly all my anger over the past few months raced directly toward him.

I walked right up to him and slugged him as hard as I could. I hit him so hard that he fell backward onto the bench with Altman. He stood up, mad as all hell, and took a swing at me. I pulled my head back, but he still grazed part of my mouth, splitting my lip. Blood splattered on both of us. Altman grabbed Chad around the upper torso or it would have been much worse. Chad wasn't finished, his anger still pouring out of him in name-calling as he struggled to get free.

It killed me to walk away from Chad, with him hurling names at me. Names that made me an outsider, made me vulnerable for the first time in my life. Not vulnerable in the small every day ways that people are accustomed to, but vulnerable in a way that was so large I couldn't yet grasp it. But I knew I had to walk away. I couldn't fight him physically, and nothing good was coming out of my staying. Renee, who must have been shocked out of her anger, tried to grab me by the shoulder as I passed by, but I threw her hand off and walked with as much dignity as I could muster to my car.

* * *

Standing by my car was my Fairy Godfather. His eyes were soft but unhappy. He took me by the shoulders and looked at me with such concern that I let him put his arms around me.

I started to cry and, as I stood there being held by him, I knew I had been angry with the wrong person. I was stupid not to see that he was trying to help me as much as he could.

"I'm sorry, really sorry. I was the one making all the mistakes. And I still am."

With a soft voice and open eyes that I could see into forever, he said, "You're back. Facing the deepest pain brought you back. Are you ready to tell your story now?"

Tears fell down my cheek and the salt of my despair mixed with the violence, still fresh, on my lips. I looked up at him, he was blurry through my tears. "I think I'm a unicorn."

CHAPTER FIFTEEN

My Own Personal Goddess

When my dad came by the next afternoon with groceries, I lied and said I tripped and cut my lip on the bathroom sink. He looked concerned but didn't say much. He did drop in more that week to check on me.

My lip was nearly healed by graduation day. I managed to avoid everyone except for Patty and Ricky, who came by and brought me soup because of my busted lip.

Patty kept assuring me that she knew I had just made a mistake and that Renee would get over it. As for Ricky, we didn't talk about it. He fixed my soup and told me not to worry, that no one would ever bother me again. I took this to mean that he threatened people with bodily harm. I didn't know if he took it personally, I mean he used to be my boyfriend in a weird way, but he never let on if it did. Bother him, I mean.

"I'm sorry if any of this hurts you," I told him.

"Those guys are jerks," was all he said.

Frances came by at sunset, like always. After I told her what happened she had this advice: "You need to be yourself—not being yourself, trying to be someone else, is what got you into trouble in the first place."

"It doesn't have to do with, you know, *that*. It's that I betrayed Renee."

She looked at me as though she might explain some Great Truth to me, but instead she shrugged.

I understood. She thought it all had to do with *that*. And I guess I knew, in some twisted way, it did. Trying to be someone, one of them, in a story that wasn't mine had been my problem all along.

* * *

I tried not to make eye contact with anyone at the graduation ceremony. I just wanted to get through it and leave for Patty's beach house. Everyone else was going to an amusement park out of town and they weren't scheduled back until dawn, so I'd have the place to myself until Patty and Gerrard dragged in. I was looking forward to the time alone.

The valedictorian was this girl named Gracie Nagel. She was nice enough. I had known her since junior high. She was giving this really lame speech about leaving high school and how much our future holds, and about how we were the future of the world. It was extremely depressing. The funny thing was Gracie herself, and how absurd her preaching was since she didn't know the first thing about living life without fear.

Gracie had every phobia imaginable: fear of public places; fear of driving; fear of animals; fear of plastic, and the list was endless. I heard that she even feared her own bed sheets and would only sleep on a bare mattress because she was afraid of getting tangled up in them and strangling herself to death. I think she probably had a fear of fear. Maybe that's what phobias were all about.

She was standing in front of the podium with blinders strapped to her head, only looking at the speech in front of her, trying to ignore the rows of graduating seniors and their proud but confused relatives. I heard they had to bring her in blindfolded so she wouldn't have an anxiety attack. But that could have just been a rumor.

After she finished her speech, she fainted, falling right into Monroe's arms. It was really quite a dignified faint, kind of like what an old-time movie actress would do, and I couldn't help wondering if Gracie had been practicing for weeks, trying to get that faint down just so.

Monroe dragged her away and handed her over to some guy in a white coat. When he came back, he started reading off names, and we got up row by row to take our diplomas. It seemed like it took forever but finally it was over. We were presented as graduates and I threw my hat up into the air. I threw it as high as I could, hoping for a big gust of wind to come along and take it to China, or at least someplace interesting.

Ricky made his way over to me and we hugged. It was like a goodbye in a way. I knew I would see him again, but it would never be the same. I don't know how I knew this, I just did.

I saw Renee talking to Patty. She looked odd dressed in blue, wearing a uniform just like everyone else. It wasn't like Renee to tolerate such ritual and conformity. But Renee was never herself anymore. She was withdrawn and tired looking, as if she'd endured a sound beating and finally said Uncle.

Diane walked up and said something to Patty. Patty nodded and left, leaving Diane and Renee alone.

Diane looked wild, untamed and free, and it was Renee who now looked reserved and unsure. Diane was talking and, apparently, said something Renee didn't want to hear because Renee crossed her arms. But Diane kept talking like she was trying to convince Renee of something. Finally, Renee said something back, shrugged in a defeated way, and turned her back on Diane. Renee's eyes accidentally met mine for a moment, those huge sad eyes, before she turned away from me with determination.

"Why don't you go talk to her?" Ricky asked.

"It won't matter." It was up to Renee to forgive me, and I knew there was a possibility she might never do that. Plus, I wasn't done beating myself up for it.

"I've come to say goodbye." Frances appeared out of nowhere. She was dressed for her trip, her graduation gown in her hand. "My bags are packed, they're in the car." She shrugged. "Time to go."

Ricky walked off to talk to some other people, but really it was because he knew I wanted some privacy. He has always been very kind in that way.

I couldn't control my tears, though I wanted to, I wanted to be strong and supportive. "God, I'm gonna miss you." I lost the battle and tears welled up and over, streaking down my cheeks. Tears for all the people I had loved. Nearly all of them, now, lost.

Suddenly, Johnny Netti grabbed us from behind and twirled us both around. It made me laugh and feel good for a moment, and I was so thankful to him for that. I knew his girlfriend must have been around somewhere, but he must have said fuck it, because he kissed us both on the cheek and told us to take care of ourselves.

After Johnny left, I told Frances to write me—that it was important. And I knew it was, because it felt like my entire existence relied on knowing I would get a letter from her. Then, for the first time ever, I felt what the restraint of expression was like—a harmless dog that only becomes vicious once it has been muzzled.

"What's wrong?" she asked.

"I want to kiss you goodbye, and I'm pissed off that I can't."

She smiled, put her arms around my waist, and kissed me. Right there, in front the entire graduating class, their parents and our friends. And it was not a peck, something that might be mistaken as girlish friendship. When we were done, she looked at me very closely with piercing intimacy and deadly serious words, like a soldier risking life and limb to deliver a vital message to the frontline. "Don't ever let people hold you down. They'll try to convince you what's comfortable for them is what's best for you. Don't believe them, Ella. If you do, you'll never be sure of who you are."

She let me go and picked up her duffel bag. She walked away with such dignity, such an air, that royalty would have salivated.

My own personal goddess.

I witnessed her walk on water, part the waters, as she moved effortlessly through the common folk, away from me, and onto something beyond us all. And walking behind her was an apparition—the spirit of a thirteen-year-old girl who drove her father's truck through town to survive her childhood.

People stared at me, their mouths agape. I tried to muster the same dignity as Frances, but I found myself not looking right or left and heading straight for Patty.

"Frances Riley kissed you," Patty said with real astonishment.

"Yes, she did. Can I have the keys to the beach house?"

"What? Oh, yeah. Here."

"Thanks."

I marched toward my car. Heads turned and I concentrated on holding mine higher. I could see my father and his stupid girlfriend in the bleachers, but I acted like I didn't see them even though he was waving to me. Did he see Frances kiss me? I didn't think so, but, honestly, I didn't give a shit what the hell he thought. What the hell difference did any of his fucked-up thoughts matter to me? He was putting the house up for sale and I would be expected out by September. No matter how pleasant he was to me, I knew I was just a responsibility to him. An obligation he couldn't legally be free of until I was out of high school. I felt a sort of bruise on my heart that I couldn't keep touching because it hurt too badly. I pushed him out of my thoughts, shut and locked that door forever.

I was almost through the entire crowd when I noticed I had to walk by Chad Walker. I hesitated. I thought he might still be mad enough to take another swing at me. I turned my resolve into armor and walked toward him. He saw me coming and stared me down, purposely trying to intimidate me. But I gave away no fear and met his eyes sternly. I walked right past him. I tensed, ready for a blow, but none came.

As soon as I cleared the crowd, I started to shake. I ran as fast as I could run, until my face burned and my lungs ached. At my car I doubled over to catch my breath. Itching at the corners of my mouth was an unexpected smile.

CHAPTER SIXTEEN

The Complicated Hero

Once I was at the beach house, I built a fire, sat in the armchair and stared at it for a really long time, but without really being aware time was passing. It was one of those moments where time is suspended, or where your time seems different and slower than everyone else's—like everyone else was at the amusement park and their time would be measured quickly, by roller coaster rides and hamburger lines.

I turned off all the lights in the house. The only light left was the glow of the fire. It was the first time I was ever completely alone in a place other than my home. There was a feeling of peacefulness about it, and I knew this was a part of my life that I was looking forward to: time and space that was mine and bent to my will.

I needed to sort things out and decide what to do with my life. I knew I would leave town, I could no longer live there. It had become a forest without light and I had become what people saw me as, not what I aspired to be. Leaving town was a given. Perhaps I would go to LA? But would I go to school as I had planned, or get a job and an apartment? I always thought, before, that I would go to school. Now I wasn't so sure. I needed time to think about who I'd been…who I'd become. I was no longer the same person. The new story had taken root.

There was a lot of stuff like this in my head when I fell asleep in the chair.

* * *

I woke up when Patty draped a blanket over me. It was morning.

"Hey. What time is it?"

"Early. We just got in. Go back to sleep. We're going to the back bedroom and crashing."

"Okay. I'm gonna get up and fix something to eat. I'll be quiet."

I went into the bathroom and threw water on my face and brushed my teeth, slapped my face a few times. I went to the kitchen and cracked a few eggs into a pan and, when I looked up, Renee was standing in the doorway. I didn't know what to say, and I didn't want my eggs to burn, so I kept working on my breakfast. Only I was so nervous that my eggs were now scrambled instead of over easy, which I preferred.

"Shit."

"What's wrong?"

"What's wrong," I repeated, laughing ironically. "It's just…I didn't want scrambled eggs."

"Oh," she said, as if scrambled eggs were some serious problem. "I'm here because everything between us is so unfinished."

"Yeah, well, I can't argue with that."

She fiddled with her hands. "The thing is, I don't really know what to say."

Neither of us could break down the stubborn wall that separated us. I tried to think up a neutral subject. "So, when's the baby due?"

"I had an abortion this morning." She smiled weakly, clearly out of nervousness.

"Oh, Renee." That's when I noticed how pale she was and a horrible wave of sadness washed over me. "Are you all right?" I went to her and tentatively reached out. She fell into my embrace and crumpled in my arms. We sank to the floor and I held her as she fell apart.

"I couldn't go through with marrying him. I don't even know what I want to do with my life. What was I supposed to do, Ella? Support us with my painting? I just didn't know what else to do." She sobbed into my neck.

"It's okay." But, even as I said it, I imagined a little child who looked just like Renee and a horrible bout of nausea hit me. Pain flooded my heart and I could only begin to imagine how Renee must have felt. It wasn't that I didn't understand why she did it, I would have done the same thing in her position, but I'd never seen a fork in the road so clearly nor so vividly felt the loss of a path not taken.

She pulled herself together and touched my cheek because I was crying too. We sat in the doorway facing each other.

I couldn't take having something between us anymore. "Look, Renee, what I did was wrong. I keep thinking of ways to explain away what happened, but the bottom line is that I did what I did. There's no excuse. All I can say is that I'm sorry. I just want your forgiveness...more than anything else in the whole fucking world."

Renee wiped her eyes and looked up at me. "Why did things have to get so screwed up?"

I looked down at the floor.

"I'm not the Queen of the Realm, Cinderella."

"What's that supposed to mean?" I was completely confused.

"I'm not the person you made me up to be. You saw me as this Rebel Queen, this Empress that ruled the realm, and as long as I could see myself through your eyes, I believed it. Then you left me alone, and I didn't know who I was anymore...I was so lost."

I couldn't believe what she was saying. Was she saying I invented her? "Come on, Renee. I don't believe that."

"Why? You saw it. And deep down you know it's true. Jesus, Ella, didn't you ever wonder why I stayed with Altman? 'The great Empress putting up with a jerk like Altman?'" she said sarcastically. "He was a flake. Did you really think I didn't know he was going out on me? I knew it. I just didn't care until it was with you."

I turned away. "I don't believe it," I whispered. But even as I said it, the truth sank in.

"Ella," Renee said, and she reached out to hold my hand. "I'm not the person you think I am."

This was incomprehensible to me. How could I have loved only an image? A false image at that? What had we been to each other—friends or illusions? "Well, what about me? Aren't you disappointed? I'm not who you imagined I was either."

"No. You'll always be the same Ella to me—the knight in shining armor. I know you."

"You don't really know me. Who I've pretended to be is bullshit, and you know it. Come on Renee, don't make me say it. I know you've heard all the rumors."

She looked away from me and sighed.

"Come on," I said, "be fair." I wanted her to really see me. I wanted her to see that the mythical creatures were real and that I was one of them; that I had been cavorting with them in disguise and that now I was removing my cloak. That I would no longer hide and that I would not run for the shadows at the edge of this world and hide in fear.

"All right." She looked at me. "I know. But it scares me," she said with a small measure of shame. "I don't want you to be closer to another girl...closer than you are to me."

Funny, that never occurred to me. But thinking about it, I understood the fear too well. "There's this weird pleasurable pain in the way I care about you, Renee." The thing I most needed to tell her seemed inexplicable. "I just know that you'll always be a part of me. This little piece of me no one else can have."

Renee buried her face in her hands. I didn't know if she was crying or not, but I had my nerve up, so I said the one other thing I most wanted to tell her. "I have to get this out so it doesn't haunt me, or something. You probably won't want to hear it and

I'm not sure about it because, well, shit, I don't know enough yet to be sure about these things, but…" I stopped myself from blabbering and gathered my courage. "I think I might have, sort of, I don't know, I guess maybe, might have been sort of in love with you." It came out in the barest whisper. I looked quickly down at the floor, immediately regretting I would never know her expression.

I heard a car pull up. It gave me a reason to put distance between us and I got up and walked to the window. I saw Diane pull up in her VW bug. When I looked back at Renee, she was looking at me with an expression that I couldn't really read, except that it was kind of self-satisfied but also afraid and timid.

"I love you, Cinderella. I never loved Altman more, or any better, than I love you. Love, in-love, I honestly don't know how to tell the difference. Maybe I'm just a coward."

I thought I should be pleased by this admission, but all I felt was let down.

I looked back out the window. Diane got out of her car and walked toward the water rather than the house.

"Maybe we love the wrong people," I said. "And it's all one huge joke on us."

"How can you ever tell who the right one is?"

Looking at her, I realized the truth was that I had no idea who the right person might be. I didn't understand this story at all.

Renee's eyes were large and vulnerable, innocent like a child's. She was no longer the Queen. "Will we stay friends?"

She was so susceptible to damage at that moment that I tried to joke her out of it. "If you can forgive me for being someone else besides your knight in shining armor." My smile faded. There was always too much fucking truth in jokes.

She stood up and walked over to the window where I was standing. "I never expected you to be that simple."

"True, but you expected me capable of it," I said, still trying to joke.

"Well, aren't we all?"

"I guess so, but I'm certainly finding it less and less tolerable. I want to be the complicated hero. Does that sound selfish?"

Renee smiled, lifting a little of the darkness that hung over us. "You still have to forgive me for being a flawed Rebel Queen. How do I know you'll even like the mild-mannered, boring, every day Renee? Overall, I'm not very exciting."

"Renee, that was you I saw doing crazy, brave things. Not some alien pod twin."

She seemed hurt. She turned her back on me and when she turned back around, she asked, "Then why should I believe there's a part of you that I haven't seen? A part you've hidden from me?"

"It's not the same thing, Renee. I had to hide my secret, at least until I understood it myself."

"So did I," Renee countered.

"But why? I don't see why you couldn't have told me how you felt."

"Because, at first, I didn't realize I was relying on your belief in me, in how everyone saw me. Then when I figured it out, I *did* try and tell you, but you didn't want to hear it, Ella. I'd try to tell you I was scared, and you'd just get mad at me."

The memories came back. I could remember, clearly, my frustration whenever Renee doubted herself. I remembered actually being filled with anger. "Damn, I'm an idiot. I didn't understand. I'm so sorry." I felt awful, like I wanted to just keep on repeating my apology, hoping it would heal it all. "I guess I did know something was wrong, but I couldn't deal with it. You were just so, I don't know, everything I admired. I guess I just couldn't handle that changing. If you were the queen, then I could be the knight. And then I knew who I was, that I had a purpose. I was wrong. I trapped you because of my need. Renee, I'm really sorry I wasn't there for you. I was wrong and I won't do it again. And I like you for who you are. I do know you, you know. I really do. I'm so sorry."

"It's okay," Renee said gently, nervously pulling at the ends of her hair. "Anyway, the truth is, I knew about you too. I could have said something, but I didn't."

I got scared and defensive. "Like what? Gee Ella, I think I should mention, since you clearly don't have a clue, that you're kind of a lesbo, faggot, queer." I intensely hated what I said, the way I said it, and wanted to take it back. It wasn't really how I felt. It was also the first time I ever said anything identifying me as gay and I regretted how negative I made it sound.

Renee winced at my words. "Please don't feel that way about yourself."

"I guess I don't really feel that way. I'm just a little scared. Do you want to know the only negative thing I can ever remember being said about gay people? It was this guy at school. I didn't know him, but someone said something about gay people and he said he didn't *believe* in *it*, like *it* was something mythical that didn't exist in the real world. I never forgot that because it was such odd phrasing. It was as if he was saying, 'I don't believe in unicorns.' So I've been thinking about unicorns. If they existed today, what would our human thoughts be about them? Some people would not want to know unicorns existed because it would scare them, it would be too different. Some people would want to conquer and cage them so they could be master. Some people won't want to share their world with unicorns, or maybe create a conspiracy that unicorns are evil and plotting to take over their world. And some people will love them because they will appreciate their beauty. And all I keep thinking through all of this is: *I'm the unicorn*. I feel like this mythical creature stuck in the human world. My world suddenly feels more complicated than it used to be. Well, I did say I wanted to be the complicated hero." I shrugged, trying to be cool and indifferent.

Renee softened, everything—her eyes, her voice, her posture. "I think you are a beautiful unicorn and I've always wanted to have a unicorn as a friend."

That was the exact moment that I knew I hadn't lost Renee, and that I never would throughout my entire life.

"We make excellent friends. We are steadfast and loyal and simply stunning to look at."

We laughed and, for the first time during the conversation, we were the old friends we used to be.

Renee looked out the window and saw Diane sitting near the water. "I'm going to lose you to her, you know."

I studied her face before I answered because I wanted to understand exactly what she meant, but all I saw was a sad surrender. "That's not how it is, you know? It doesn't have to work that way." But part of me wasn't so sure. I mean it wasn't like I knew what I was doing.

"I wish you were right." She was silent and then added, "She asked me to come talk to you."

"Is that the only reason you came here?" I felt incredibly pained at that possibility. It must have shown on my face.

"No." Renee looked over her shoulder at me, reassuring me with a firm gaze. "It was my excuse."

"You didn't need an excuse."

Renee gestured out the window. "She wants you to go to her, you know."

I looked at her expecting sarcasm, but all that was there was sincerity and uncertainty.

She laughed.

"What?"

"You're blushing."

"Jesus, Renee. Knock it off."

"Sorry."

I decided to change the subject. "So, what are you going to do now?"

"I'm going back to the school to paint a new mural. It will be my last victory over Monroe."

I laughed, imagining Monroe's frustration. "Actually, I meant in life, what are you going to do with the rest of your life kid?"

"I don't know. Painting the mural's first. Maybe I'll discover who I am...something between the Rebel Queen of all I survey and a mediocre human girl. What about you, fair Cinderella? Where will all this take you?"

"The only thing I know for sure is that I'm moving away."

She looked down at her shuffling feet. "Will you keep in touch with me?"

"Oh, Renee," I said, exasperated. Emotion was balled up like a fist in my chest. "I wouldn't know how *not* to keep in touch with you."

A moment later she was hugging me, whispering in my ear. "I love you."

"I love you too."

Just as quickly, she relaxed her hold on me. I knew she wanted me to do the same, but it was so hard. When she pulled away from me, her cheeks were dark with color and her eyes were cast down. She pushed hair from her face in an effort to compose herself and reached for a casual tone. "So, I'll talk to you in a few days. You weren't going to pack up and leave tomorrow, were you?"

And that was it. It was over. "No. I have to actually have someplace to go before I can leave."

The tone of the conversation became typical. We became, like always, the same two best friends whose hellos and goodbyes were as predictable and commonplace as the ocean tide.

I watched her walk out the door. From the window I stared after her as she drove away.

Life was more bizarre and sad than I ever anticipated.

* * *

I walked down to where Diane was sitting watching the waves break. She felt my presence and smiled but didn't look at me.

"I saw you kiss Frances Riley."

"Yeah, I think everyone saw that."

"Are you two together?"

"I don't know actually. I guess we were, for a while. She's leaving for the Peace Corps."

"Oh." Diane siphoned sand through her fingers. "Do you wish she was still here?"

"I don't know. It's not really about that..." As I talked, the realization came to me. "She rescued me when I really needed it, that's all. I'll never forget that."

"I wish I could have been the one to rescue you," Diane said regretfully. "I missed my chance. Now someone else has won Cinderella's hand." She tried for humor, but it fell short because of the real regret she felt. She rested her chin on her knees and closed her eyes.

"That's an old story. Who cares about it? Make your own story. I am. I'm sick of trying to fit into some old story that doesn't feel like the truth."

Diane looked at me out of the corner of her eye before looking away again. Neither of us said anything. I was bothered that she wouldn't look at me. "Why won't you look at me?"

"I can't. That's too dangerous."

I smiled in spite of myself. "Gee…I'm so flattered."

My goofiness made Diane smile. "Look, I came here because I really want to spend time with you, be around you. I understand if you don't feel the same way, and I'll leave now if you want me to. Just tell me the truth, do you want me to go?"

"I can't lie to you, I'm not some majorly stable person. I'm still confused about most everything in my life right now—"

"You mean people?"

I knew she meant Renee, not Frances.

"But I really, really don't want you to go. Please stay," I said.

I knew she was tired of competing with Renee and she looked, at first, like she might say no, but then she looked at me and said, "I'll stay. For now."

When I smiled at her, she looked away.

* * *

Gerrard built a fire for the night and Patty was in the kitchen fixing dinner. I was amused by this and thought of Patty and my vision of her life as a warped *Gidget* episode. Diane was curled up in one of the armchairs, a blanket covering her legs. She was reading a book she'd pulled off one of the shelves.

I was sitting at the table, losing at a game of solitaire. I kept sneaking peeks at Diane. I suddenly realized that it was really damn hard not to look at this woman. Especially sitting there by the firelight. Her hair was so carefree with its wayward curls, her skin so milky, her eyes so large and expressive—Jesus! She could have been a fucking Disney character. It wasn't normal to be that beautiful.

I was startled by my conscious ramblings. What the hell was I doing? This was new, this conscious admiring and craving. And I'd referred to her as a woman. Everything felt so strange, this crossing of invisible boundaries that were designed to change me forever.

Diane looked up at me as I was pondering her. I knew I was caught red-handed, but I didn't look away. She stretched and put her book down.

Now, how can I adequately explain that when she performed that one small gesture, how this huge want came forward, without restriction or shame, and how there was no doubt anymore as to what I wanted? Dear Christ, the things I wanted to do to that Disney-looking woman. It just wasn't right.

"I think I'll take a walk," she said and looked at me in all her non-Disney innocence. "Want to come?"

I put down the cards and walked out the door with her. From inside the house Patty yelled after us, "You're coming back for dinner aren't you? It'll be ready in an hour!"

We ignored her and walked out onto the sand. I wanted to let Diane know how I was feeling, so I reached out and laced my fingers with hers. Our palms touched and my stomach filled with ticklish air.

She stopped in her tracks, halfway between the house and the water. I could see her face in the moonlight as she looked down at our joined hands and then up into my eyes. "That's not enough anymore."

I moved her hair aside and put my hand on the back of her neck.

And we kissed. We kissed like in a fairy tale, the sexiest, most romantic, raunchiest, most beautiful fairy tale ever. Hard and furious, soft and slow, hard and furious, soft and slow, keeping time with the tide.

* * *

We found a small soft sand area surrounded by rocks. Not the same place we were *That Night*, but a new place, where new memories could be made.

We shed our clothes, and were rather flippantly brazen about our nudity, and whether anyone would discover us. I was really coming into my own when Diane, out of breath, stopped me from making love to her.

"What's wrong? I did something wrong, didn't I?"

"No," she said, pulling my face up to hers. "I'm just a little nervous."

This surprised me because she was so sure of herself these past few months. "But I had the impression that you've done this before."

"I have."

I looked at her with a baffled expression, not understanding.

"Do you have to be hit over the head with a brick? I'm nervous because I'm with you."

"Oh." A blush crept up, coloring my already aroused flesh a deeper shade of red. I stretched out beside her and played with her hair. "Do you know how long I've been dying to touch your hair?" I rubbed the curls in my face, smelling her. "And your skin." I ran my finger from one shoulder bone to the other, then down between her breasts. "And your lips." I touched those lips that always looked so swollen.

"Okay," Diane said, "I'm ready."

It was that moment, when lips moved delicately in opposite directions, creating gentle friction, over and over again until it was excruciating, until there was no other trail but the one that led to surrender and, once she gave me that, I entered and took what she offered. Oh, sweet release, when she laid down her shield and I claimed the cherry from her tongue.

* * *

We spent the night in the second bedroom making love. I wanted to imprint myself on her body like a branding iron, and I wanted her to mark me as well. I wanted a lot and expected a lot. I have heard people say that lovemaking is an art. A phrase easy to skim past, or dismiss as ego, but I thought that maybe it was true.

And since all art must have something to say, an emotion to express, it was not the trail of a tongue or the stroke of a thigh, or when to be tender, or when to show passion, those were merely brush and technique.

It was a truth to be conveyed. A dance. A description. So long as it was something that needed saying. And so I felt sorry for the lovers in the world who had nothing to say, but who held their schooled brushes so skillfully. I would rather in fumbling childlike scrawl create what must be said, than with refined patience and craft create that which has no true story.

Also, the bedroom was much better because sand didn't end up places you'd rather not have it.

* * *

At some point, in the early morning, I got up out of bed and sat in the rocking chair near the window. The moon was completely full and I could see the waves hitting the shore. I'd woken up thinking about Renee, a disturbing dream of some sort that escaped me after I was fully awake.

Light fell upon the bed and I could see Diane clearly. Her hair fell over both pillows and the white sheet just barely covered her, one arm thrown above her head. The curve of her so much like painted art, so much like a deadly curve in the road. I envisioned myself lying next to her. It was interesting, and I thought about that for a long time. I would turn, and so would she. Sometimes facing each other, sometimes reaching for each other…sometimes turning away. And there were no shadows. I could see it all clearly, even in the dark.

Making love to Diane was very different from being with Frances. It was complicated, and being with Frances was so easy and without worry for the future. This delicate creature affected me in a way that Frances could not—so why did I hold back? Regardless of how innocent and vulnerable she appeared as she lay there, I saw the dangerous attachment I had already made to her. There were going to be strings. There would be love. Passion. Jealousy. There would be fights and making up. I knew

I would love Diane with a great hunger, and that it was not going to be easy.

And sometime that morning, after the moon and before the sun, between my wanderings and my aching, I wondered if could I love Diane, like I should love a lover, without losing Renee.

CHAPTER SEVENTEEN

Falling into Deep Slumber

I was watching Diane before the knock on the bedroom door came. At that moment, in that room, I suddenly felt nothing. All there was...was nothingness. An emptiness that carried some fertility, which is exactly what the possibility of both life, and death, most felt like.

I reached out a hand to move the hair from Diane's face just as the knock came.

"Just a minute." I shook Diane awake. Her eyes popped open and she quickly sat up and grabbed a shirt. I wasn't able to get a shirt myself before Patty was in the room. Her face turned so pale that I thought she might faint. She must have thought the same thing because, once inside, she slid down the wall to the floor.

Diane was standing now, buttoning up a pair of shorts. And if Patty's face was bone white, Diane's was blood red. She was embarrassed as hell that Patty had walked in on us.

With the sheet pulled up to my neck, I looked at Patty and was about to really let her have it when I noticed she was crying.

She took a deep breath and in a shaky voice said, "Ricky just called. Renee's in the hospital."

Diane stopped buttoning her shorts. "Why?"

My chest was tight and I held the sheet closer to me.

Patty could barely get the words out of her mouth. "She was beaten up."

"By who?" Diane was incredulous.

Patty looked at me. "They think Altman did it. His parents heard a gunshot. They found him in his bedroom, shot in the head." Patty half sobbed and covered her mouth, trying to control it. "Ricky said he killed himself."

Diane's legs couldn't hold her anymore and she sat back down on the bed.

Nothing on me, or in me, was working. Never had I sensed such fully enveloping darkness before. It fell over me with paralyzing force. I couldn't stand. I couldn't speak. I could barely stop myself from sinking back down into the pillow and falling back down into a deep slumber.

Diane's hands were shaking. "Why? Where?"

"They found Renee by the mural at school. I guess someone in the neighborhood heard them fighting. It was around two o'clock in the morning."

"Is she..." I tried to ask about Renee, but there was something so large in my throat that I couldn't make sounds.

Patty answered me anyway. "She's in critical condition, that's all Ricky could find out. We'll drive back just as soon as you guys get dressed."

Diane looked at me. I could still sense the remnants of her embarrassment buried under everything else. I looked away. I felt some irrational guilt springing into my eyes and I didn't want her to see it so I covered by reaching for a shirt.

* * *

We drove in silence. Patty drove and Gerrard sat next to her. Diane and I were in the backseat.

I didn't sit next to Diane the way Gerrard did Patty. I didn't hold her hand, or rest my head on her shoulder. Not because I was afraid to in front of Patty and Gerrard, and not because I thought Diane would be embarrassed. I could feel how much she wanted my touch. She reached out a tentative hand and placed it over mine, but I couldn't seem to look at her or acknowledge the gesture. When she could take it no longer, she pulled away.

And if you think I didn't feel bad about that, you'd just be *dead* wrong.

But I couldn't touch her anymore because I knew I had betrayed Renee again. I knew, in the deepest part of my heart, that if I had really pushed it, it would have been Renee sitting here with me. Not Diane. Renee would have stayed with me last night. She would be safe. She never would have gotten hurt. I should have continued being Knight to the Queen. It was my job to protect her and keep her safe, and I failed.

Because somewhere, deep inside, I must have wanted Diane in this way more than I wanted Renee—I just knew that was it—and then I felt guilty for not loving Renee good enough. I felt like I'd fucked up royally. And all of this came rolling at me as pure emotion. I can't adequately explain the overwhelming guilt—it poured into me, through me, bubbled over and coated me like a thick, bad-smelling vomit.

* * *

We arrived at the hospital just as Mr. and Mrs. Hammond were coming out of Renee's room—Mr. Hammond had Mrs. Hammond by the elbow and was maneuvering her away. Mrs. Hammond looked lost, devastated. Once she saw me, she came up to me and took my hand. She told me to go see her and told the nurse I was her sister so I could get into the room. I don't think the nurse really believed us, but she must have decided to have a moment of decency because she let me go into the ICU. Mr. Hammond firmly reestablished his grip on his wife's arm and pulled her away from me and moved her down the hall. I couldn't read him. At first, I thought he was just angry, but it was more than that—he was removed emotionally from caring about his daughter, it was as if there was some disgust in his face.

When I got to her room, I just couldn't go in, so I stood by the door. Her head was wrapped in gauze and she was hooked up to a bunch of machines.

She wasn't conscious or anything, so it's not like I could have talked to her anyway. Finally, when a nurse gave me a dirty look for blocking the doorway, I went in and sat on a chair at the end of her bed. I don't know exactly how long I sat there and looked at her. It's not like she was doing anything. I just stared at her. Just looked and looked until this feeling came over me and everything started to fade out and go dark. Then there were flashes of light, like really dinky lightning. That's when I knew my world was shattering. I knew it instantly. The splintering of glass pierced my eardrums—the wetness, my lifeblood, and my oxygen, poured out and away from my gulping mouth like I was a beached fish. I felt air invade my pores, all my orifices. It hit me in the face and burned my eyes, touched me all over with this vicious dryness. The feeling of nakedness was intense and perverse.

I came to with a nurse standing over me. It was the one who had been annoyed with me. Her face was kinder now, but there was no color. She was all black and white, her mouth working like a silent movie.

CHAPTER EIGHTEEN

Buried

It was late June and everything in the whole world felt hot and sticky. The wind stirred up dirt that stuck to my sweaty skin. Even my sunglasses were no good. The damn sun was so bright that they merely stopped me from going blind, but not squinting like hell.

With everything in my life now gray and muted, shadows and light were even more pronounced than before. For instance, the dirt was a lighter gray than the railroad tracks I was walking along. I looked up and saw a black dot move across a dingy, slate blue sky. I was already so tired of seeing gray.

I stopped along the part of the brick wall that was across the street from the mortuary. Of course I couldn't go to Altman's funeral, I would never give him that kind of respect, but I couldn't seem to stop myself from walking over. I think it was partially because I wanted to tell him how much I hated him.

I closed my eyes and imagined the casket and the hypocritical mourners inside. A lot of the people who went didn't even know him—they just went to school with us. That's the funny thing about teenagers; death intrigues them even as it freaks them out. You hit them with it at the right age and they'll go to their worst enemy's funeral.

I closed my eyes and saw them all in there. I imagined Altman's graduation picture, or his football picture, or some real saccharin thing that would make him look like this real swell guy, a real how-could-an-All-American-boy-do-something-like-this? kind of thing. I closed my eyes and told him, right to his false face, "I hate you, you son of a bitch. I hate your fucking guts."

Still, part of me felt strangely sad about the whole thing. I felt really sorry that anyone had to be hurt. Even that Altman had died. But I wouldn't let myself think that for too long.

Besides, I think it had less to do with him than my general curiosity about why it happened. Why did he do it? Nobody really seemed to know, and the fact was that since he was dead, nobody seemed all too fired up about figuring it out. After all, he was the problem and now the problem was gone. Teachers, parents, society at large had all lucked out—no one needed to get their hands dirty.

I crossed my arms along the top of the wall and rested my chin there. I felt the heat of the concrete blister my skin, but I didn't move. I liked the sensation, the pain. It made me feel, and I was afraid I was on the verge of never feeling again. And that's what Altman had been, a damn unfeeling machine. Or was he? Would a machine kill itself?

When Chad Walker, Zip and the rest of those football guys came out of the double doors carrying the casket, I didn't think I could take how cliché it all looked. All black and white, with their poorly fitting suits and short haircuts, like a rerun of an old fifties movie, like tonight they would rumble to exact revenge on the gang who killed their brother.

I lay my head down on my arms and closed my eyes.

When I looked back up, I saw the hearse pull out of the drive and turn onto the street. Other cars started to follow.

That's when I felt a rumbling. It was a few seconds before I actually heard the train whistle. My feeling of being dead changed into a sensation like bugs in a maze trying to find a way out from underneath my skin.

I saw the train round the curve of the tracks and knew I didn't have time to move. I pressed myself against the wall and anchored myself there by wrapping my arms over the cinder block wall.

I held onto the wall as the cars flew past me. I was no more than six feet away from the train as it violently sped by. Wind and gravel beat my face and body. I held onto the wall for my life, as much from the emotional battering happening on my insides as the dangerously high winds threatening to suck me under the locomotive.

My sobs punched my bruised innards harder than the wind and flying dirt pummeled my raw flesh. I wanted to howl up into the sky.

When the train passed, so did all the emotion inside me. Immediate stillness followed, like a still lake within another still lake. The emptiness was drowning me.

I slid down the concrete wall and looked down the tracks. One direction went into town and the other way went out past the city limits to open space and mountains. I looked at this scene with my new black and white eyes and all I wanted to do was walk down those tracks, follow them out of this place, to wherever they led me.

I heard the crunch of gravel and my heart lurched.

"I thought that was you."

I recognized Ricky's voice right away. I can't say I was really glad to see him, but I still smiled.

"Can I ask you a question?"

"Sure." He sat down next to me.

"What was Altman's story?"

Ricky looked at me, trying to figure out what I meant. Then it seemed to click and he said, "Mom, dad, brother, sister. Mom stayed home. The father was gone a lot on *business.*" Ricky finger-quoted the word business. "It was kind of messed up because sometimes he'd take Altman with him to meet the women. And then Altman would have to keep the secret too."

"Jesus. Didn't he feel bad for his mom?"

"I don't know. Whenever I was around, he always just seemed like he hated her. I think he wanted her to stand up for herself, but she wouldn't. She was really submissive, like she was a servant, not a wife. Man, my mom would kick my dad's ass if he did something like that."

"Yeah."

We just sat there, not talking, just baking in the sun like the gray rocks.

I thought about Altman and how he'd had his story shoved down his throat just like I had—all written out for him. But there must have been some part of him that wanted to reject his story as badly as I wanted to reject mine, otherwise why pick someone like Renee? She wasn't meek, or submissive. Maybe he thought if he picked her it would change his story. But it didn't, because he couldn't resist the lure of that story, and he still tried to make her fit into it. And maybe she would have if it weren't for everything coming out like it did and Renee standing up for herself. But that didn't fit into his story at all, so he destroyed the whole damn thing, just blew it to bits. If he would have just had the courage to really change it.

What was the difference between him and me? It was just a matter of degrees, wasn't it? Some small, maybe, seemingly insignificant moment, where you decide not to follow the story anymore, and you stray just a little bit until you find yourself all alone in some landscape you don't recognize, and instead of running back to the same old safe story book pages, you wander, you become an adventurer, an explorer, and you revel in it even though you're afraid because it's your adventure and not one that someone else planned out for you.

"Do you need a ride?"

"Yeah, I want to go home," I said.

CHAPTER NINETEEN

Owned

I wasn't at home all that long when Patty called me to say that Renee finally woke up and was, apparently, freaking out.

It was nearly a week since it all happened and I hung around the hospital most of the time. Every day, I watched her just lie there, and I started to think this was it…that was all she was ever going to do.

I drove to the hospital as quickly as I could.

As soon as I got there, I understood what Patty meant. I heard Renee yelling from down the corridor and I ran the rest of the way.

At first I just saw the back of Patty and a couple of nurses. Every time one of the nurses tried to touch Renee, I could hear Renee scream, "Get off! Get off!" When I stepped closer, I saw that Renee was wiping away the nurse's touch like she was wiping a poisonous spider off her arm. I knew it was because she couldn't see, that's why she was so scared. Her head was wrapped and though her eyes were open, it was obvious that she couldn't see anything. Hell, anybody in her state would have been scared.

The last thing she probably remembered was Altman. And now here she was in some strange place, not knowing what happened to her, not being able to see anything.

Her speech was garbled and it was hard to make out what she was saying. She allowed Patty's voice calm her. "It's just a nurse. You're in the hospital." Renee sort of relaxed but not enough to actually let one of the nurses touch her without throwing a fit. Then I saw that she'd pulled out her IV, and that's what the nurses were trying to fix.

Patty saw me come into the room. "Renee, Ella is here."

Renee stopped thrashing about and sat real still. "Ella?" She said my name again and started to sob. She reached out her arms and cried my name again.

"It's me. I'm here."

She grabbed my arm and I actually thought she was going to try and climb on top of me. She was so desperate that it was like she was naked—in that way that embarrasses people. The nurses sort of looked away, like they could deal with their patients' most private bodily functions, but not their most private emotions.

I said, "It's all right," over and over again, but she scooted up the bed and curled herself into a ball and was clinging to me for dear life. Finally, I crawled up onto the bed and put my arms around her. She was crying so hard, and it was so weird because of how her eyes were so blank.

"You're in the hospital. You're safe. No one can hurt you again," I told her.

"He'll get me," she whispered and held on to me tighter.

"No," I said. And maybe I took a big chance telling her this, because Patty looked at me with fear when she knew what I was going to say, but I did it anyway. "He can't ever hurt you again. He's dead, Renee. He's gone forever."

Her whole body relaxed a little bit. Not altogether, but definitely some, and I knew I was right to tell her.

I told her the nurse was going to put the IV back in, and Renee went ahead and let her.

* * *

I was with Renee the next day when the doctor came to visit. I guess, since Renee was eighteen, they didn't have to wait for her parents to be there. It was strange, this line we all silently crossed over into our adulthood.

Renee held my hand and waited. I had already been informed about her condition while she was unconscious. Everyone knew, but no one had been able to tell her because of her emotional state.

The doctor stood next to the bed, studying her chart. He was a slick-looking old guy with his white jacket over expensive clothes, watch, cufflinks, tie clip—the whole shebang. "We believe there's a good chance that you'll regain some vision on the right side of both eyes. But if you don't regain vision on the left side of both eyes, that will be a permanent condition referred to as Homonymous Hemianopsia. Since the trauma occurred on the right side, here," he touched the back of her head, "it will affect the left side of your vision in both eyes and that vision is more compromised. Does that make sense?"

Renee nodded and squeezed my hand tighter.

"When you were admitted, we operated to stop the bleeding so there would be as little damage as possible."

"But I can't see anything at all," Renee whispered.

"That's because the swelling hasn't gone down yet. We hope that once the swelling goes down, you'll regain at least partial vision." He said it as though he were proud of himself.

"Is there any chance I'll get all my vision back?" Renee asked.

"Well, there's always a chance you'll get more back than we anticipate. These things can be unpredictable. We'll just have to wait and see."

"For how long?" Renee asked.

"Excuse me?" he asked kind of absently while he wrote something on a chart.

"How long until she knows?" I asked. He was sort of getting on my nerves.

"Oh, I'd say about three weeks at the earliest. Maybe four. After six months it's unlikely there will be any further improvement. Any more questions?"

Renee shook her head.

The doctor was looking at his watch. "Hmm?" He prodded her.

"She said no," I answered.

"Fine." He turned on his Italian shoes and walked his arrogant ass out of there. I swear to God, as soon as he hit the hallway, he began to whistle.

* * *

I don't know how Altman beat her. It wasn't just with his hands, that I knew, but I just couldn't ask, or even think about it, because I literally believed my heart would stop beating and I would just die from the violence of it. Nobody gets that kind of head injury, three broken ribs, and a fear like I've never seen, at the bare hands of another individual.

* * *

Weeks passed. Everything felt jumbled and I was tired all the time.

Whenever I left the hospital, Renee had anxiety attacks. The nurses broke the rules and let me hang around with her until she fell asleep. At night I'd slip away from her and go home, but she'd be impossible until I came back the next morning.

I was actually getting used to hospital food, which honestly wasn't as bad as I thought it would be. Maybe I had low standards.

One night I was lying in bed with her and I dozed off. I usually didn't because then I wouldn't know when I could sneak away. Anyway, I felt a feather moving across my face, across my lips. I woke up and saw Renee lying next to me and I remembered that I was still at the hospital.

She was touching me. Delicately allowing her fingers to move up and down my face. It reminded me of her soft touch when she painted, so delicate but precise. And it was so raw, just so incredibly raw, and I wondered how much longer I could take it without whimpering. I made myself lie still and not breathe. I didn't want to interrupt her, but when I couldn't take it anymore, I laid my hand on top of hers.

She jumped a little, startled, because she thought I was asleep. She placed her hand flush upon my cheek. I held it there with my hand.

"I want to see you again," she said. "I miss your face. I miss looking at you. You were always mine, my sweet Cinderella." She gently pulled her hand away and ran it down my neck to my shoulder, then down my arm and back up. She felt my collarbone down to the half moon crevice.

I started to get nervous, but I kept silent. She moved her hand down to my breast and taking it in her palm, circled around it. My stomach jumped into my throat when her hand traveled down my stomach and over my hip. Her leisurely touch was painstaking, like she was reading me, knowing my shape. Knowing me differently than before.

She journeyed to my inner thigh, and with the slightest pressure, urged me to let her in. When I opened to her, she held me there, cupping me gently, almost possessively. She stayed there for some time, not moving around particularly, not trying to get me all hot, just, I don't know, like she couldn't get close enough to me. Like she had to touch me as intimately as possible. That's when I felt the bubbling of desire in her breath, released quickly, hot in my ear.

It was like a switch, that moment, a charged surge of influence that's passed from one person to another.

My breath mimicked hers and she moved her hand up to mine, took hold of it and placed it on her face, encouraging me to touch her and know her. But, to tell you the truth, I just couldn't do it. I touched the gauze on the back of her head and where they had to shave the surrounding hair to operate, and honestly, it was just so damn sad that something snapped in me and I started to cry. Renee touched my face, felt my tears, and she started crying too. Her body was heaving and her lips were pulled down sadly. And I realized, looking at her now expressive face, a face that was usually private and secretive with tall castle walls surrounding it, that her mouth was what I wanted most, it was what I had always wanted most.

I leaned over and kissed her. I tasted salt, either from my tears or hers, and it wasn't much of a kiss because neither of us could breathe very well from crying, but I just kissed her fiercely, a whole bunch, over and over again, trying not to sob as I did so. The kisses became fewer once we caught our breath, blending into one kiss, and I read her as though my lips and my tongue were my fingers and my eyes. I read her just like she had read me. I read her like one does a long-forgotten childhood story. But now, with both of us all grown up, nothing about the story seemed the same.

Her kiss was shy, but trusting, and just so damn tender. The sweetest kiss I've ever had in my life. It made me understand her, really know her. I saw how small she was and how easily hurt. It made me want to cry all over again. I broke the kiss so I wouldn't sob. I held her to me and pressed her face into my neck, because now I could touch her in secret ways, the way she had touched me. And I held the cherry passed from her mouth into mine, cradling it protectively, sparing it from the mashing of my teeth. I would protect that delicate cherry for the rest of my life.

Finally, she moved her hand to my waist and she held me there, but not just in any old way, it was like after you've made love to someone and you have this real ease with her now. Because after you make love to a person you can touch them freely, and that's how it was with Renee's hand on my waist. Like, in her way, she'd just made love to me.

That night I stayed until the sun rose, at least for my eyes.

* * *

I kept spending days and nights with Renee. One day sort of just melted into the next without any real significance.

The only real difference was that, after that night, Renee touched me like I belonged to her. Her touches were more intimate, like she'd have me sit on the bed and hold her, and not just because she was scared, but for her pleasure, because it felt good. Sometimes she would even kiss my neck. And she'd reach for me anytime she wanted to hold my hand, like I was her girlfriend. I mean, *girlfriend* girlfriend. I mean like a lover.

All this would have all been fine and dandy with me, but what concerned me was that it was accompanied by this *need*. This need that felt...wrong...somehow. What concerned me even more was that she simply wasn't functioning in anyone else's presence but mine.

Actually, I was beginning to worry she was flipping out.

CHAPTER TWENTY

Seeing Eye Dog

I stretched out my arms and extended my fingers. I was in that place where you're not all awake and you still think if you wish hard enough that your dreams will solidify.

I was having this really great dream about Diane. She was leaning over me and her hair was all over my face and her golden eyes were electric and at half-mast. It was so great. You know how dreams can feel so intense, with a desire like nothing you've ever known and it makes you want to close your eyes and go back to sleep, because how can you wake up to reality after that? Besides, what was really cool was that the dream was in color. Weren't dreams supposed to be in black and white?

I rolled over and moaned. When I looked at the clock it was after ten.

"Damn it! Son of a bitch! Shit! Fuck!" I fell out of bed just as my vocabulary level reached a new low. I cussed all about my room as I tried to dress. I was trying to put my socks on, standing up and jumping in place, when I realized: I couldn't do this anymore. I sat down on my messy, post-erotic bed.

My life was slowly turning into a disaster movie. I was sure an earthquake or towering inferno was just around the corner.

I knew Renee was counting on me. She was scared. In her shoes I would have been too. But Christ-on-a-pony I was tired. It had been nearly three weeks. Every day I was with her from sunup to way after sundown, and she wasn't getting any better. Her physical wounds were getting better, but that's not what I mean. Her mental state, damn it, was no better at all. She was just getting more and more dependent on me.

Okay, I have to cop to the fact...shit, this is hard to admit ...I guess, in some way, the entire time I'd known Renee, I'd always wanted her to need me. I mean, I thought she was it. I—God—I idolized her. An idol needing you? An idol loving you and wanting you more than anyone else? But now she was helpless and really needed me. And I had to admit that it was becoming too much. It was high volume and out of control. It made me wonder, who was the person I loved? Was it this vulnerable Renee? Or was it only the Renee who was brave and crazy? The artist and politico? Was I that fucking shallow?

Well, I didn't have an answer for that, so I showered and left for the hospital.

I stopped at the mailbox. I include this minor detail because I finally got the letter I was waiting for. It was strange to look at because, for one, it was from outside of the country, but also because it was the first time I'd ever seen Frances's handwriting. The letters were long and proud just like she was. I held the letter to my cheek, imagining her as she put the letter inside, licking the glue and sealing it. Did she turn it over and look at it longingly, thinking of my skin, before letting it travel the distance to me? I saw her doing it. I felt the paper between my fingers before folding it up and putting it in my pocket. I would read it when I had time to appreciate it.

When I got to the hospital, they were in the middle of relocating Renee to another room. Renee, as you might imagine, wasn't too happy. She was up at the top of her bed, holding her pillow close to her chest like it was some type of barrier between her and the world. The nurse was trying to coax her into the wheelchair.

Patty was standing on the other side of the bed and Gerrard was playing a game of solitaire on Renee's bedside table. If the scene seemed blasé under the conditions, you can see that the whole deal was wearing thin on everyone's nerves. Patty, even the nurse, looked bored with Renee's refusals.

When Patty saw me, she smiled and waved even though she was exasperated. "Hey chick, where've you been? You're late for work."

Well, I did have to smile at that.

Gerrard waved hello and went back to playing cards. Renee perked up and reached out her hand to me—now a very familiar gesture.

"Ella..." She waited until I took her hand. "They want to move me to another room." She whispered, "I don't want to go somewhere else. I know where everything is in here. I can get around. Will you talk to them please?"

She rubbed my arm as she talked. I'm not complaining about that, mind you, but she had the strange idea that since she couldn't see, she could do these things and no one else would notice.

Of course they did.

Patty raised her eyebrows at me, a kind of *ahh-look-at-this!* She meant it as a joke, as a tease, but it still made me feel embarrassed.

I guess I forgot to answer Renee because she asked me again if I would talk to the nurse. "I'll see what I can do," I said.

But it wasn't going to be easy. The nurse was a tough, battle-scarred older woman who appeared as though she'd seen a war or two. She gave me a tired look and said, "Come on, let's get out of her royalty's earshot."

She was kind of right, the way we'd all been milling around her, like we were her court. And we always were, so why would anything change? It made me sort of sulk out the door after her. Actually, I think I was just having a really low day. I was having a hard time just lifting up my head.

"We're moving her to the psychiatric ward," she said.

That made my head jerk up. "What? Why?"

She looked at me sarcastically. "Are you serious?"

"How is that going to help her? She's just scared. Wouldn't you be scared if you got the shit beat out of you? If you were in some strange place for three weeks and couldn't see a thing? Not knowing if you'll ever see again? I think you'd be pretty fucking scared!" Now I was yelling at the nurse, and I knew that wasn't helping matters. All right, I was also yelling at myself. I needed to remind myself what it was that Renee was going through. I was feeling like a real shit for being tired and wanting it all to end. "Come on," I pleaded now. "Come on, she doesn't need to go there."

The nurse wasn't too happy. I could see she thought I was way too young to be throwing *fuck* and *shit* right into her face. "You're not doing her any good babying her like you do," she said in a firm voice. "She's got to stand on her own, especially if she loses her sight. Unless, of course," she said, mocking me, "you plan on being her Seeing Eye dog too? Now, I'm telling you, the only way that girl is going to get better is if she gets some help for her mind. We've done all we can for her body. If you really are her friend, you'll help her now when she most needs it. So, what's it going to be?" She stood with her arms crossed waiting for my reply.

I think part of me wanted to pop her a good one for being such a shit about the whole thing. I mean, for her it was just another day at the office, but it was my damn life she was cutting down to size. But, I have to tell you, another part of me blessed her for it. I was so relieved to be told I needed to let go. "All right," I conceded, but at least I pretended to begrudge them their solution to Renee's problems.

When we went back into the room, Renee was relaxed and talking to Patty and Gerrard. She just knew I'd take care of her and fix it all, and that trust in me did make me feel I was doing this all begrudgingly. I still wasn't completely convinced a shrink would help her. All I was convinced of was that I wasn't.

"Renee, I need to talk to you."

"Come on, Gerrard. Let's go get something to eat." Patty and Gerrard left me alone with her. The nurse stood near the door.

"I talked to the nurse and I think it might be a good idea if you went with her."

"Why?" And she was so genuine—she really did want to know why I thought so. I'll tell you, her trust in me was choking my heart black and blue.

"Because I think you need some help. You're not getting any better. You need to talk to someone who can help you not be so afraid."

She held my hand tightly. "But I'm not afraid when I'm with you."

"But I'm not helping." I felt like I was going to cry from sheer frustration, but I held back.

"You're going to leave me with some doctors and not come back?" It was disguised as a question, but it was really a statement of fact.

"No," I protested, but then I realized I didn't know what would happen, so I amended. "I don't know. If they'll let me, I'll come here every day, you know that. But, right now I'm not helping, and someone has to help you. You don't want to keep being afraid forever, do you?"

She didn't say anything.

I hit her with the big one. "Renee, what if one day you're afraid and I'm not here? I can't be here every time."

She loosened her grip on my hand. For a moment I thought she might pull away from me, and under normal circumstances she would have, the Renee of before wouldn't have liked appearing this dependent upon someone. But instead she tightened her grip on me. "Okay."

I nodded to the nurse and we helped her into the wheelchair.

* * *

Well, here's a real hoot. Even though everything was about as serious as things could get, all I wanted to do was howl with laughter.

When we got to Renee's room there was Gracie Nagel herself, lying in the other bed, her trusty blinders strapped to her head. I tell you it stopped me in my tracks.

The nurse was busy getting Renee situated in her bed and good old Gracie lifts herself up on her elbows and swings that clunky head of hers around. "Hey, I've been expecting you."

"Gracie," I said it loud enough for Renee to hear, "what are you doing here?"

Okay, the real question was why didn't she live here?

"I have to check myself in when my anxiety attacks get too bad." She smiled.

She had a really nice smile and I realized what a nice person she was. The whole time I'd known her she'd always been pleasant and just generally decent. How many people can you say that about?

"I talked the doctor into putting Renee in here with me. Since they know me here, I have some pull."

I walked over to her so she wouldn't have to strain to see me. "Gracie, do you mind if I ask you why the..." I pointed to indicate her blinders.

"Not at all, a lot of people ask me. I just get scared when things come at me from the sides, like they're sneaking up on me. This way I control more of what I see, so I'm less afraid, you know, less likely to have an anxiety attack." She explained it so easily, so confidently that I was having a hard time imagining her afraid of anything. Plus, she was our class valedictorian. She was incredibly nice and not bad looking. It seemed like she had so much going for her. What could she possibly be so afraid of?

But just then, Gracie's eyes popped out of her head. She was panicked and cowering. "No!"

I saw a nurse approaching her with some bedding. She stopped cold when she saw Gracie freak.

"Not the sheets!"

The nurse who was helping Renee ran over and pushed the other nurse out of the room. "Not her! She has a phobia. Get out of here with that." Both nurses scurried out of the room, and I mean literally. I noticed Gracie was lying on a bare mattress.

I backed away from Gracie, now curled into a ball and turned away from me, her body quaking.

"What's going on?" Renee reached out for me.

I took her hand. "Just Gracie. She freaked because the nurse brought in some sheets."

"What?" Apparently Renee hadn't kept up with all of Gracie's phobias.

"Nothing. She just got scared, that's all."

"Like me." Renee said it really mean, like she just hated herself.

"No, not like you." I rubbed her hand for reassurance.

Renee leaned toward me. If she could have looked me in the eye, I know she would have. "I don't want to be like that."

"You won't be," I reassured her. But frankly, I wasn't so sure and I was happy to hear her say it.

Patty and Gerrard found us. "There you are! It took us two floors to track you down," Patty said. She looked over at Gracie who was still shaking.

"Is that Gracie Nagel?" Gerrard asked.

"Wow, it sure is. Hey ya, Gracie. How you doin'?" Patty asked cheerfully, as though the other girl wasn't in the middle of a major anxiety attack. But if you knew Gracie, you would understand that you just had to do that. I mean, all around school you would find Gracie in the middle of some kind of anxiety trauma: in the bathroom, in the gym, sometimes just sitting by her locker in the hallway. She had a terrible time of it. It got to the point where people just sort of ignored that she was freaking out. I mean, you have to understand, it just wouldn't have been polite to ignore her, or freak out yourself, so people just started saying, "Hey ya, Gracie."

I sort of respected that she never gave up going to school.

"Ella, I thought I might relieve you for a while if Renee doesn't mind putting up with me. What do you say, Renee?" Patty asked.

I was dumbfounded by the suggestion because once you've been doing something for that long, no matter how much it might be wearing on you, you just can't imagine not doing it. "I don't know." I knew I wanted to take her up on it, but I wasn't sure how Renee would take it.

"I didn't ask you, I asked Renee. So, Renee, do you mind? I think Ella has a few things to do. Some errands, or something, right Ella?"

Obviously she wanted me to go along with her, so I did. I felt like the girl being led around by the end of her nose today. "Yeah, I have a few things."

Renee either cracked under the pressure, or maybe (and I really hope this was the case) she decided on her own. Anyway, she let go of my hand. Just like that. Even though I knew it couldn't have been that easy. "Okay Patty, we can play cards. You can tell me all about the hand I've been dealt." The double entendre was lost on no one.

I have to admit that I panicked for a moment. I wanted her back, her reliance on me.

"Well, you better be on your way," Patty needled me.

I lightly touched Renee's hand goodbye and she smiled but didn't grab hold of me. She clasped her own hands together until her knuckles turned white.

I got up and as I walked past Patty, she whispered in my ear, "I think there's someone who really wants to see you."

Of course, I knew she meant Diane. I felt embarrassed about that. I had not handled that well. I'd checked out on her in this really big way. "I know."

"She doesn't know what to do," Patty whispered. "You're not returning her phone calls. I told her you've been here the whole time, but still…"

"Yeah, I know." Have you ever felt really small? This was working into a real shit-ola of a day. "I'll see you later."

"Where?"

"Back here."

"I don't think so." Patty pulled me all the way to the back of the room. "This is it. She's not having any visitors after today. We're only being allowed here during the transition."

"*What*? No one told me this!"

Patty shrugged.

"Well then I'll stay here until they make me leave."

"No, that's why I'm here. They know she's too attached to you. When I leave it won't be so bad, being as I'm only her second best friend." Patty's self-deprecating remark was supposed to make me laugh. It didn't. "Ella, she has to get better. She's too dependent on you. It was bad enough before, but now!"

"What do you mean before?"

"I mean before."

"You think she was dependent on me?"

"Please! You didn't know that?"

Boy, was I confused. "No, I never thought so."

"Well, remind me to tell you about it sometime. Right now, you have to go." Patty pushed me toward the door.

I took one more look at Renee.

I'd seen her everyday for the past month, now I was wondering when would I see her again.

CHAPTER TWENTY-ONE

How Water Should Taste When You're Thirsty

It was around noon and the sun was frying everything to a crisp. I saw a mirage of water as I walked out of the hospital. The sun, as hot as it was, felt good to me, but then, just as quickly, it began to make me feel nauseous, probably from coming out of the air conditioning.

I leaned a shoulder against the side of the building. It was made of rocks. Maybe they were red and blue, I guessed. Or maybe green.

I touched the rocks. They soaked up the heat of the sun and were burning hot to the touch. I pulled my hand away instinctively, but then, just as instinctively, I drew my palm near again. I visualized my palm scraping across the jagged surface until it bled. I had this idea that it would be interesting to watch the blood seep from my body. I walked down the steps to a patch of grass. There stood a tree and a bench. I sat down and tried to figure out how I felt.

I felt lost was how I felt. I didn't know what to do now that I was relieved of my duty to Renee.

I looked down at my feet and saw a few blades of grass pushing through the cracks in the concrete, and for about two seconds, I just wanted to laugh.

"Are you ready to move on?"

I must have really been out of it because there was my Fairy Godfather on his motorcycle, revving his engine. I didn't even hear him pull up. I looked at him, but I just couldn't talk.

He smiled and patted the seat behind him.

I got up from the bench in what seemed like slow motion.

* * *

I tilted my head back and closed my eyes. The wind on my face and the movement underneath me was brilliant. I was in love with that ride. Leaning into the turns was like defying gravity. I opened my eyes and looked out at the grassy fields. Everything was in vivid color: blue skies, green grass, brown dirt and black pavement—so simple, so primary, so beautiful. When tears came to my eyes, they were kissed away by the wind. I wrapped my arms around the black leather jacket in front of me and pressed my cheek to it as I watched the color whiz by.

* * *

I skipped stones and thought of Frances. My Fairy Godfather was lying in the shade of a walnut tree. I looked at each stone carefully before I threw it. The blue of the water and the eventual plunk that caused the white splash made me unbearably happy. I didn't think I could stand how peaceful I felt, but that peace also made me want to burst. I didn't ever want to leave the lake.

I took off my pants and walked into the water in my underwear and T-shirt. It really didn't bother me to undress in front of him. Something had sort of crossed over in me. The truth was that I've never been uncomfortable in front of guys. It was girls who made me nervous. Though I like the private discomfort they brought, the way it eased into pleasure, I despised public interactions such as gym class and locker rooms.

The coolness of the water, I can't describe it exactly, except that it somehow made me understand why I was alive, like my whole existence was designed simply so I could be in that cool lake at that very moment. It wasn't something that made sense when you said it out loud, but rather only when it was inside you. I wouldn't have been able to tell him about it because then it would have gone away.

I leaned my head back to let my hair get wet and slowly submerged my whole head. When I came back up, he was in the lake too. He was completely under the water, his face up toward the sky, his cigarette sticking straight up like a marker of some sort. I leaned my head back too until my ears were submerged. I could hear a soft continuous thump, as if the lake had a heartbeat.

I don't know how long we floated there. Long enough for his cigarette to burn down. He put it out in the water then threw it onto the shore. I noticed what a beautiful face he had. Soft features, though the beginnings of a beard covered up his jawline.

He noticed me looking at him. "What?"

"I'm sort of disappointed you aren't magical."

"I'm incredibly magical."

"You know what I mean."

"No, not really," he said.

"Well, that means either you're crazy or I am."

"That's the problem. There's no magic because you don't believe it's possible. If this were an old fairy tale from several centuries ago, you would believe it. If it were the future, or another world, you'd believe it. But present day signals crazy, right?"

"Yeah, pretty much."

"It's because you don't accept the magic within yourself. I'm the part of you that's pure magic, that can lead you to your happy ending."

"Come on, there's no such thing as happy endings. Besides, I can see you. I can touch you." I pressed a finger to his cheek and his flesh indented. He was real. What was he talking about?

"Plus, I know that you just nosed around and found out about my past. This stupid town is so fucking small." I looked at him carefully so I could gauge his reply. I wanted to know the truth.

"You're just avoiding the reason I'm here."

I knew what he meant. I wasn't even going to pretend I didn't know. It was all about Diane. It was always about Diane. I put up every roadblock imaginable on my path to her, but I still ended up at the same crossroads to that story every time.

I leaned my head back and took a deep breath. I submerged myself underwater, slowly letting air out. I sank lower and lower toward the bottom of the lake. I could feel the muddy bottom on my feet, squishy between my toes.

A tightening around my arm pulled me upward and, in a matter of seconds, I broke the surface. My Fairy Godfather looked at me with those stoic eyes of his.

I had two fistfuls of mud. I smeared one handful all over his hard face, and laughed at his surprise, before unloading the remaining sludge. He looked ridiculous with his cool expression all covered in mud. It cracked me up and I just totally lost it. All the tension in my body from holding myself together for Renee popped, like a balloon filled to its bursting point, and I laughed for the first time in what seemed like forever. I couldn't stop. When a little smile cracked on his face, that was it, I mean it, it was exactly what I needed—just to be free completely, no more serious talks, no more life or death situations.

Once I got him to laugh, I started a big splash fight that went on until my arms ached. He grabbed me by the wrists to stop it once we were both completely out of breath, but that reminded me of the way Frances had always stopped our splash wars, and it broke me in some way. With all the tension gone, the problem was right there in front of me, like a small little caterpillar inching across a wide, busy two-lane highway.

"What if because I chose Diane, what happened to Renee happened?" I asked, my voice cracking.

And I sobbed.

I never in my life sobbed the way I did at that moment. I fell forward and he wrapped his arms around me while I disintegrated. Everything I had been up to that very instant fell away. I was naked and alone in the world.

"You're not alone," he said. "I'm here."

I don't know how long I cried, but eventually he led me out of the water. He laid down his leather jacket. On the inside it was lined with soft, quilted material. He motioned for me to lie on it. I plunked down on my stomach. He sat next to me leaning against the tree.

"Even though your mom was crazy and wrong, she was your mom and you loved her, right?"

I rested my forehead on my arm and stared at the quilt pattern on his jacket. Did I love my mom? I guess before a heart can break, love must be there first. "She was my mom. I thought she had to love me. I didn't know she could take it back."

"No child thinks that. We expect they will love us. It doesn't occur to us that they have the option to leave us. Thinking a mother's love is permanent and unconditional is what gave you the courage to stand up for yourself, to demand to be seen, to be brave enough to tell your story the way you wanted to tell it, not the way she wanted it to be. But when she broke that promise to love you and to take care of you throughout your childhood, she broke your belief in your story. But you can't forget the courage it took to stand up and say this is me, this is the story I'm telling."

Tears were streaming down my cheeks. I couldn't look up at him. "And look where that got me."

"It got you here, today. The only thing is you know what your story is supposed to be, but you're still trying to push it away."

"I don't know what it is. I'm confused."

"Search your heart. Are you really confused? When you became Renee's Knight and swore protection for her, you created a safe haven for yourself and for her. Who knows which of you decided upon this story—Cinderella, Knight to the Rebel Queen. What difference does it make? Maybe you both participated in the creation because you needed it to survive. Either way, it served its purpose: you both survived. But now what? The story is over."

"But if I leave the story, what if she doesn't survive?"

"It's not your role anymore. It's time for her to find herself. She needs to find the story she belongs to—this isn't it anymore. Prolonging it is just hurting her. It's also hurting you. Cinderella, you acted so bravely when you chose not to sacrifice your story for your mother. Are you really going to sacrifice it now for the Queen? For a story that no longer even exists? You are telling the story past its ending."

"It's Diane I want. It's always been Diane. But I'm scared. Do you think I've lost her?"

"You already know the answer to that."

* * *

It was a vivid day. Maybe color had only left me for a while and now it was back for good.

My Fairy Godfather dropped me at home. I went to the oak tree and opened the letter from Frances. It was there, leaning against the oak tree we made love under, that I read her first letter to me. It was a little strange. The voice I was so used to was different in the letter. She always seemed more together than anyone else I knew, but now, she seemed more thoughtful than ever before. In fact, she seemed damned well wise.

The beginning of the letter was more formal than I was prepared for, but still very loving. Once I thought about it, I realized that was sort of how Frances was. Then I reached this part of the letter that was just really *it* for me. I don't know why exactly, except maybe it was because it helped me see her there, and that made me long for her.

And the sunsets, Ella! I wish you could be here with me having a glass of iced tea and eating sunflower seeds. The sunsets, they're orange and purple and magenta. And when I see them it doesn't matter to me anymore that you're so far away and I can't touch you or wrap my arms around you. Do you understand? I'm not telling you this to offend you, but because I want you to understand. I wake up in the mornings so awake and I go to bed so sleepy—and here I sleep on a hard cot. At home I had a queen-size bed and a warm, clean comforter (I'm sorry I never had the opportunity to share that with you, but the oak tree was much better anyway). It's strange to me that I had to leave behind everything that was comfortable in order to know how a glass of water should taste when I'm really thirsty. Do you understand, Ella? I just know you will.

I don't want to make it seem like it was all roses. A good part of the letter was about the rough times she'd been through. She was sick her first week, and was harassed by some of the local workers. But this was the part of the letter that moved me, the part about the sunset, and all. It made me really understand her, and I knew that's what she wanted from me. I understood how she was telling me about leaving what's safe, how necessary that is, even though you're not unhappy with it, or anything like that.

She had to go. I could see that.

If she hadn't left her comfortable bed for a hard cot, she wouldn't be seeing sunsets like that.

In some way, I saw that it was sweeter for her to remember how we made love than to stay here and try to make it keep happening. That would be lame because it would have died out, it never would have lasted. It was a lot better this way. She was willing to let the old stories go and let the new stories begin.

Still, I remembered her there with me under the oak tree. I lay there, in the spot where I used to see her looking down at me, and closed my eyes and imagined her there. Touching me. Kissing me. Pulling my pants down over my hips. Her hair touching my face, my neck.

But it wasn't Frances's face that I saw. It was brown wavy hair and golden eyes with a shy smile. It was the face that I saw in my dreams every night.

I got up, my heart beating like crazy, and I hopped the brick wall, right past Frances's ghost. She was sitting there cracking sunflower seeds between her teeth. She smiled at me as I passed by her and ran down the street.

* * *

I'm not going to pretend that I didn't know where I was going. All the same, I didn't think about it much while I was walking. I let my mind go hazy, like a fog had rolled in, and I just walked to where I most needed to be.

The sun had set completely, and it was dark by the time I reached the white-planked house. The light from Diane's bedroom was spilling out onto the green grass. She was nowhere to be seen.

There in her front yard was a cherry tree. I probably wouldn't have noticed except that many of the cherries had become too ripe and were now lying all about the yard. I picked one up from the ground and gently rolled it between my forefinger and thumb. It burst and the juice rolled down my fingers. They were black cherries and this one left my skin looking bruised with its purple blood.

I reached for a cherry from the tree. Most of them were still very firm. I pulled off a few. The ones that were too firm I threw on the ground for the birds. I don't like those. I preferred the ones that were right on the borderline. Not yet rotten, like most on the ground, but nearly, right on the verge.

I found one. It was tender and juicy, I could tell by rolling it around between my fingers. I wiped it off on my shirt and popped it into my mouth. I let it roll around on my tongue for a while before I broke the skin, bleeding out the sweet juice. My saliva glands produced more spit than I thought possible. I chewed the meat between my teeth, tearing it away from the seed until it was bare bones.

Cherries right before they're about to go bad are the sweetest.

I saw Diane come into her room and just stand there in the middle, not doing anything really. She walked toward her bed, but then changed directions and stopped at the window to look out.

I hid behind the tree. I knew she couldn't see very much, it was too dark and there was no moon. When she went to her desk, I came out from behind the tree.

I walked over to her window and watched her sit there with a pencil in her hand, staring at some paper but not writing anything.

Having a brief flash of courage, I tapped on the window.

She looked over at me. I knew she could see me because I was right there at the window. The light from her room must have illuminated my face, but she turned away and looked back down at her paperwork.

I was going to tap again on the window, but just as I lifted my hand to do so, she looked at me again.

She walked over to the window and slid it open.

"Hi," I said.

She didn't say anything, just looked at me.

"Will you come outside?" I asked.

She didn't say anything. Didn't move.

"Please," I half-begged.

She looked at me, I mean deeply, to see if I really meant it. She climbed out the window and walked past me to the cherry tree. She stood there with her back to me. I circled around and faced her.

"I'm sorry," I said.

She looked at me. "That's just not good enough anymore."

She told me that at the beach house when she wanted me to kiss her, so I leaned toward her and took her neck in my hand to pull her toward me. I saw her golden eyes glass over before she pushed me away.

I didn't want to lose her. I couldn't stand the thought of it. I reached for her again. She pushed me away. Again, I reached out for her, like a dog that can't stop loving even when they're getting kicked. I just couldn't stop. I thought I might start crying. I could hear myself begging.

The next time I reached out to her, she pushed me up against the tree and held me there. She kissed me and held my hands against the bark. I felt her bite my neck and winced at the pain, but it also made me feel crazy when she whimpered and let my hands go. I wrapped my arms around her and she kissed me hard. Different from any way it was with us before. I pulled her to me and guided her hands to my body. With every move of my body, I gave myself to her completely. She only resisted for a moment before she surrendered to what I wanted and she opened my pants, ripping the fly in her haste, and entered me quicker than I would have thought possible.

It didn't hurt. The opposite. I was so ready for her, ready so long ago, so lovesick for her that I had to hold on to her tightly so I wouldn't fall to my knees. I couldn't contain a moan into her thick, wavy hair.

Her inside me like that, making us one, I started to cry because I could feel all of the pain and hurt she had, and it was so sweet, because her desire for me was so *there*. It was just like those cherries, like I'd caught her just before everything went too ripe, too rotten. I knew it wasn't too late.

I wanted to tell her I was sorry, but I couldn't talk, all I could do was feel her and me mixed up together. All I could do was beg, please, please, into her ear. Which is exactly what I think she wanted, for me to beg for her love. She wanted me to stop lying about how I felt.

And when it was over, she didn't move. We just stayed there. I whispered into her ear, "I'm so sorry. I love you. I'm so sorry."

She cried into my neck.

She released me and slid down to the ground in despair, her face on my thigh. Headlights illuminated us as a car drove down Diane's street. I became acutely aware that all of this was happening in her front yard.

I got her to stand up and walk with me to her window. Once we were inside, I had her lay down. She turned away from me and faced the wall. I crawled onto her bed and wrapped my arms around her.

I encouraged her to turn around and face me. I began the story.

"A long time ago, there was a girl named Cinderella, but she wasn't *that* Cinderella, and so she disappointed people.

"But a day came when she found another story. One that would make her feel honorable and purposeful—she became the favored Knight to the Rebel Queen. And that was okay for a while, she served the Queen well and she was well regarded throughout the kingdom. Until the day she met the beautiful Rapunzel, and Rapunzel stole her heart. From the very first time Cinderella saw Rapunzel locked away in her tower, she knew that she would never love anyone else the same way.

"But Cinderella fought her love because she was afraid if she left the Queen unprotected, the Queen would come to harm. But Cinderella couldn't resist her love for Rapunzel, so she went to her, and in Cinderella's absence the Queen was attacked and injured.

"Ashamed at having failed to protect the Queen, Cinderella punished herself by forsaking her love for Rapunzel. But very soon afterward, Cinderella found that she could no longer serve the Queen because she couldn't live without Rapunzel. So she went searching for Rapunzel, her heart heavy and broken until she could find, once again, her one true love.

"When she found Rapunzel, she was under a cherry tree. She went to her, but Rapunzel turned her away until she saw that Cinderella had given up her role as Knight. Cinderella removed her armor and laid it at Rapunzel's feet. She swore her everlasting love as the simple Cinderella, not knight, not princess, just a girl."

And Diane returned to me. From the distance of the moon she came back to earth, she returned to me—eyes, lips and heart. And when she returned to me I was never so happy. Never. There was no day that preceded that day that ever had that much bliss. When I looked into her eyes, I saw our hearts latched together tightly and I felt such fullness in my throat. I knew then what was going to happen. I was no longer afraid as I loosened the cherry from my heart, moved it through my tight throat, past my lips and onto her sweet tongue. And that's how I lost my virginity.

CHAPTER TWENTY-TWO

So Damn Sincere

We were lying naked on my bed. Diane had a crossword puzzle on my stomach and I was reading some really corny novel I was about to give up on, where all the teenagers acted like pod people.

Diane reached down and pulled the cotton from between my toes. "They're dry."

"Now you can take it off."

She eyed me playfully. "No."

"You promised, Diane. I only let you because you said you'd take it off afterward."

She laughed, rolled onto her side and laughed some more. She was having a jolly old time at my expense. At the expense of my blood-red toes, that is. "I don't have any remover," she claimed.

I didn't buy that. I wiggled my toes. "Ugh. I feel like a prancing poodle."

That only made Diane laugh even harder.

It had been a week since I had gone to her house, since the Cherry Tree Episode. In that short time, I learned things about Diane I never would have guessed when I was just her friend.

One afternoon we were lying on the floor of Diane's bedroom. We were filling out our college applications.

"Are you hot?"

"No, I'm fine," I answered absently. "But open the window, if you want." I never looked up from my application.

"There's a spot, right where your thigh ends, right before, you know…I want to kiss you there." She scooted up next to me, her lips just grazing my ear.

"There's a spot between your breasts where I'm just dying to lick you."

You get the idea. Diane, to my utmost surprise, was very verbal. I mean she loved to talk. She'd be all the way across the room and, in no uncertain terms, would tell me what she was going to do to me.

Maybe it was all those years of cheerleading, like all intentions had to be chanted first: *Go team! Go team! Score, score, score!*

A fallen cheerleader is a gift from the gods.

* * *

Diane took me to a club-like café just an hour outside of town called Mister Hyde's. It had little tables set up all around and a pool table.

It also played host to a couple of Diane's ex-girlfriends.

It was where Diane went after what happened with us that one bad night at the beach house. The girl who was with her the night of the warehouse party was playing pool. She kept looking over at Diane.

I looked at Diane too, but she wasn't looking at the girl. She was holding my hand, turning it over and rubbing the lines on my palm with her thumb as she talked.

I swelled with pride at my victory.

Diane's fingers grazed my skin in that electric way. That's when I knew she wanted me. I looked back at the girl by the pool table.

She looked kind of sad and my pride deflated into humility. It was the first time I was ever around others with my story. I was no longer alone in the void of nonexistence.

Here were mythical creatures, same as me, with a story the world said didn't exist—not in any meaningful way, where you deserved a storytelling of your own. In them, I could see the same silent story: muted, gagged and tied up, held hostage, caged prisoners, banished, captive in a dark, dank basement prison cell. Some had tunneled out and escaped into the light of a place like this one and chose never to return.

Others, no doubt, stayed in the darkness—too afraid to leave behind their families and the world they grew up in, which they still loved regardless of their story banishment and nonexistence. But were they ever really happy?

I neither wanted to escape nor live in the basement prison.

I was Cinderella.

How could I go from the most famous fairy tale of all time to nonexistence?

It was unacceptable. It was impossible.

Surely people would notice if my story went missing? I would notice. It was my duty to the narrative to tell the truth, and if the world didn't like it…well, I would become a warrior.

If this story were meant for oblivion, I would go out of this world chivalrous and honorable. Wielding my blade until the end. Following the virtuous path of true love. In my wake, the mighty truth this story has borne.

Cinderella was not going down without a fight.

* * *

I went over to Patty's house. Her parents knew Renee's parents and I wanted to find out how Renee was doing. Patty was sunning herself out by the pool. I sat down in the shade of the big umbrella table.

"I don't know much except that supposedly she's making progress and some of her sight has come back." Patty shaded her eyes from the sun, looking over at me in concern.

"Really?" My heart lifted a little. "I wish I could see her. When will she get out of there? It's already been two weeks."

"End of August maybe." Patty shrugged. She was just guessing to try and make me feel better.

"I'll be gone by September first. I hope I can get an apartment and a job by then." I hit my thigh. "There's got to be some way I can see her before then. Isn't she going to school in the fall?"

"I don't think so." Patty looked sad when she said it.

I knew it was because that made her think of Gerrard. They were going to different colleges. They were going to try and stay together, but it would be hard. She was going to one of those rich all-girl schools. I thought that was pretty funny, considering Patty wouldn't exactly appreciate it the way I would.

"You're going to really miss him, huh?"

"I'll be with a bunch of girls and he'll be on a co-ed campus. Who do you think is most likely to find someone else?"

"Patty, Gerrard chased you around campus for years. The guy's crazy about you."

"I guess so." But she looked pretty bummed. "It's great about you and Diane—and even going to the same school? You're such a lucky shit. You've always been lucky."

Me? Lucky? I'd have to give that some thought.

"So, are you two getting an apartment?"

"I'd like to, but I doubt that will happen right away."

"What are you going to do?"

"We're getting a dorm room. But we figure if we get jobs, well, we'll see how things work out, you know."

Patty smiled at me all sincere. "I think it's going to work out great."

For some reason that I really can't explain, it felt so incredibly good to hear her say that. "Really? You think so?"

"I really do." And she was so damn sincere it just made me want to sweep her up off her feet. I hugged her really tight. I think she was a little surprised but she hugged me back. A really good hug too, not one of those fake ones, like yeah-get-away-from-me-now things. I just loved Patty. She was honestly and truly my friend.

* * *

The problem with summers is that the older you get, the shorter they become.

Two months went by at a clip.

Not being able to see Renee might have made it longer, and more unbearable, if it hadn't been for Diane. But that month I spent with Diane, before starting college, was the best month of my entire life. In some ways, it was also the saddest because of Renee, but nothing could detract from this high I felt with Diane.

I guess I have to admit: not even Renee. Perhaps the happiest and the saddest were meant to be together, two halves that weren't supposed to be separated.

And perhaps that's why when the day finally came for me to see Renee, it didn't surprise me that it was the day I had to leave for college. When I found out the date Renee was going to be released, I planned around it. I knew my life was going forward with Diane, away to school, away from this town, and I didn't want to be sucked into misgivings or trapped by my love for Renee.

I would go to her house with my bags packed. After seeing her and saying goodbye, I would meet Diane at the café in West Hollywood and we would drive to school together. If it was all planned out, I wouldn't be able to change any of it. It would be in motion. I would finally be unstuck about Renee.

* * *

We were in my room. I'd just finished packing my bags and was tying my shoes. "So, I'll meet you at Mister Hyde's."

"Okay. I'll be waiting." Diane sounded kind of funny to me.

Like she was really saying, she'd believe it when she saw me walk through the door.

"I have to go do this. I can't *not* say goodbye to Renee, she was my best friend all through high school."

"I would never expect you *not* to say goodbye to her. You're the one who's acting so paranoid."

"Well, you sound funny."

"I don't sound funny! You feel guilty!" Now Diane was mad.

I think secretly I wanted her anger. I knew it was really fear that she wasn't admitting to me, and I needed to know she was as scared as I was. But I didn't like what she said. "I don't feel guilty."

"You're afraid to tell her about us."

"I am not afraid. She already sort of knew before anything even happened. It's not like it's news."

"I'll tell you why, because you have feelings for her that aren't just about friendship. Best friends, my ass."

"Now you're really starting to piss me off."

"I'm out of here. I'll either see you there, or I won't." Diane picked up her bags and climbed out the window.

I felt all shot up. It was like we just verbally machine-gunned each other.

And it all happened so fast because it was everything we'd wanted to say, everything we'd both been thinking over the past month. There was no careful measuring of words or judgment in our delivery. We just fired deadly words with reckless abandon.

After I pouted and stewed for several minutes, I fell backward onto the bed and tried to soothe my nervous stomach. I didn't do it on purpose, I mean I wasn't looking for it or anything but I was looking around my room and I saw the Disney album from Cinderella. It was the one item connected to my mother that I could never throw away for some reason. I mean, it's not like I listened to it, I just couldn't let go of it.

I picked it up and took out the record. It was for one song that I kept it. I put the album on my stereo and selected the song, dropping the needle with shaking hands.

A Dream is a Wish Your Heart Makes. I thought I might cry, but I didn't. I felt completely calm. I realized that I kept the record because this was the part of the story that wasn't wrong. It's funny how my mom was so focused on the girlishness of Cinderella and how she needed to be beautiful to ensure the prince would rescue her. To me, when I was young, the whole story was only about this, what the song says—to not give up on your dreams. Any dream. Believe in your story, even if you're the only one who ever knows it.

I opened my suitcase and put the record in my bag. I don't know why. I took a deep cleansing breath and let it out. I knew I had to go see Renee and get it over with. I picked up my bags and took one last look around my room.

I left a note on the table saying goodbye to my dad. He was away camping with his girlfriend. We never did talk after graduation, so I had no idea if he saw me kiss Frances or what the hell he thought of me in general. Honestly, I didn't seem to be something he thought about, beyond being a chore—like doing laundry or vacuuming, basic housecleaning. You don't think about stuff like that, you just do it. Still, he put a roof over my head and kept me fed. So, as far as I'm concerned, he deserved a note.

I closed my window, locked it, and walked out through the front door.

CHAPTER TWENTY-THREE

I Promise

I saw Renee sitting on her red velvet chair, palette in hand, paintbrush in her teeth, as she studied a canvas. *She studied a canvas.* She could see.

The window was open. I was going to say something but the sight of her, with all her hair cropped so short, stopped me. I couldn't decide if she reminded me of Joan of Arc or Samson after all of his hair was cut off. It was barely over her ears.

"Hey," I said.

She jumped out of her chair. "Ella!" She leaned out the window and embraced me.

She was so happy. I couldn't believe it. What a change. I was overwhelmed. I'd just sort of assumed that she'd be moody and melancholy.

"Come inside." She motioned with all this enthusiasm.

I was stunned. "You seem really okay."

"I am," she said, but with more significance than ever before. She took her well-being seriously.

"What happened?" I asked. "You seem so happy. You look great."

She touched her hair, timidly. "I'm getting used to it. I kind of like it, actually. I might keep it this way."

I reached out and touched it. It was really cool, all soft and short.

She took my hand and had me sit on the bed with her. "It's really nice to be able to see you."

"Is it all back?" I asked, referring to her sight.

"No." She shook her head sadly, but not in any way that was sorry for herself. "I can see on the left side of both my eyes, but not on the right. It's like there's these pockets of darkness."

"Oh." I was really sorry. I expended a lot of energy wishing she would get it all back.

"It's okay. I'm learning to work around it. I'm even painting." She gestured to a couple of canvases leaning against the wall of her bedroom.

The images were spectacular. Not primary colors anymore, but influenced more by black and white and gray. But so exquisite, really. I was amazed by how much more lyrical and moving they seemed compared to her old work, which wasn't quite as soft but more bold and vigorous and ideological than emotional. And yes, there was a bit of sadness in it. "They are so stunning, Renee, really."

She held my hand in both of hers. "I want to thank you."

"What for?"

"For being here for me when I needed someone, more than I ever have. I swear, Ella, you saved my life." She touched my cheek with her hand, so I'd look at her and know she really meant it.

"You'd have done the same for me," I said.

"I know I would have," she admitted. "Probably for no one but you."

I sort of blushed then. She was making me feel like Knight to the Rebel Queen again. I knew I should fight it, but I had no defense for the Queen's charm. I suppose I never really did.

"That's also what I need to talk to you about." She got up and walked across the room. "I talked a lot to this therapist. A lot. They make you do that there. I didn't like her much at first, but I sort of got used to her. The thing is, I don't know what I am—if I'm gay, or straight. Whatever, you know. And right now, I just don't really give two shits to be honest. What I do care about is that I love you. And Ella, I've never wanted to keep someone near me, and with me, so much in my life." She brought her fist up to her heart to make her point.

I swallowed hard.

"But, I just can't."

My stomach dropped down to my toes, like when you're on a roller-coaster ride. "What do you mean?"

"It turns out that I have this dependency thing...problem, I guess...I need to try and figure out who I am, all on my own."

My ego was bouncing around the room like a rubber ball. I nervously looked around the room, my eyes landing on her bedside table and the snow globe. I picked it up and held it between my hands. "So, what are you saying?"

She looked sort of chagrined then, you know what I mean? Being called on it, now she was having a hard time saying it flat out.

I pressed her. "Don't you ever want to see me again?"

She looked up real fast. "No! That's not what I'm saying at all. I just meant—look, it's going to all work out anyway. You're going to college and I'm not starting until spring. We won't be seeing a lot of each other anyway. I just, I have to do this, Ella. Do you understand?"

How could I not? I saw what she was like. It wasn't right for a person to be that way. As much as I always loved her, I'd never been like that. "I understand. I swear Renee, I really do."

She smiled gratefully. "Thank you." After a moment she said, "I know about you and Diane. Patty told me."

That kind of pissed me off. "Damn Patty." I shook the snow globe and watched the white flecks swirl angrily around the perpetually ripe cherry bomb and the sugar-white mountains.

"Don't be mad at her. She doesn't understand how things are with us. For her everything's so simple."

"I wanted to be the one to tell you." I wondered if it hurt her.

She must have read my mind. "The truth is, Ella, I don't even know if I have a right for it to bother me. I mean, what are we anyway? We're friends, right?"

I shrugged and smiled. Some sort of huge boulder rolled off my shoulders and I felt like I could breathe around her for the first time in months. "Yeah, we're friends."

She walked back over and sat down next to me. "Friends forever. Okay? Promise you'll be my friend forever. Not Knight to the Queen, not anything other than who you are, who I am— just you and me. Do you promise?"

"Yes. I promise."

She took the snow globe from me. "You always did like this." She shook it before pressing it back into my hands. "You keep it. So you never forget me."

* * *

Before I left town, I drove to the railroad tracks. I sat on that wall across the street from the cemetery and looked down the train tracks, at the way out of town, toward the flat plains and the mountains I would cross over to meet Diane. I turned my back to the mortuary, my high school and the house I grew up in. The train tracks were steely silver and the sky was like a giant blue lake you could swim across. I was gone. No matter how many times I would come back here in my life, this was the moment I left this place forever.

And there, walking down the tracks was my Fairy Godfather in his ripped and safety-pinned jeans and his spiky green hair. He turned once and waved to me. I didn't know if I'd ever see him again. Maybe he was moving on to the next town to help someone else. I don't know. I waited for him to sprout wings and fly away, but he didn't. He just kept walking down the tracks.

* * *

I walked into Mister Hyde's and saw Diane before she saw me. She was facing away from the door, like she didn't want to have to watch for me. Like maybe her faith in me, in her future, would be enough. I tell you, it's the small things like that that can make you really fall in love with a person.

I walked around to the other side of the table and sat down. Diane looked at me and down at her coffee. I reached over and held her hand.

Still looking at her coffee, she said, "That's nice, but it's just not enough anymore." When I laughed she dropped her tense shoulders. I noticed she was holding something in her hand.

She set a key down on the table between us.

My heart rose to my throat and softened my voice. "What is this?"

"A key to our apartment."

"We have an apartment?"

"We do now."

I picked up the key.

"I thought you might not come. I knew that if I was lucky enough to see you again, that I would say I'm sorry for getting mad. If I'm the one, all you have to do is tell me and I'll believe you."

"Diane, I'll tell you if you need me to, but you know this is our story now. You know it in your heart. I just had to close the book on an old story, that's all."

"I know." She reached over and held my hand. "Please live with me."

"But I don't have a job yet."

"So, we'll figure it out."

I was buzzing inside. Live with someone? I'd always been so alone. Waking up with Diane there. What would that be like? I was scared, but I wanted to try it. "Okay."

"You know how the last line of that old story ends, right?" Diane asked, her golden eyes smiling at me.

"Tell me," I said.

"And so Cinderella and Rapunzel lived happily ever after."

"But wouldn't that mean that's also the opening line to this story?"

"You're going to make this complicated, aren't you?"

I settled back in the chair and looked at her. Had she learned nothing about me?

Bella Books, Inc.

Women. Books. Even Better Together.

P.O. Box 10543
Tallahassee, FL 32302

Phone: 800-729-4992
www.bellabooks.com